Heroics

Heroics

George Alec Effinger

OPEN ROAD

INTEGRATED MEDIA

NEW YORK

ISBN 978-1-4976-4008-5

This edition published in 2014 by Open Road Integrated Media, Inc.
345 Hudson Street
New York, NY 10014
www.openroadmedia.com

For John and Eileen Kandrac, in return for their elder daughter. Further, Mr. and Mrs. Kandrac will receive an undisclosed draft choice and a nice thank-you note.

The soul is born old but grows
young. That is the comedy of life.
And the body is born young and grows
old. That is life's tragedy.
—Oscar Wilde
A Woman of No Importance

Chapter One

A Fateful Breakfast

Irene hadn't always been dead.

She remembered that she had lived a very long and very full life. She was grateful for the opportunity she had been given. As she floated in the blackness she recalled one incident after another, things that had happened to her, things that had made her happy or sad. She had enjoyed life, and she wished that she could personally thank whatever had made it possible. If the old men in California had been right, Irene's wish would come true. She was doubtful, though. The empty blackness that surrounded her seemed as infinite and unchangeable as anything she had ever experienced. She was dead, and death was empty and unchangeable. The old men in California had tried to persuade her that there was more to death than that. Irene was doubtful.

She hung in the void and thought. Without sensation, without even the sense of her own body's existence, there was nothing else to do. Irene thought back to the morning that had begun the sequence of events leading to her death and her present occupation: floating. Dreaming.

Irene remembered that morning very distinctly. It had been early spring, the second week in April. The trees had begun to show the first pastel hints of the dark forest-green leaves to come. The day was Irene's birthday, her eighty-second. She was happy about it. She loved birthdays, her own and those of her family. Every birthday was a reason to celebrate—not her own defiance of mortality, but the wealth of associations that had grown over the years. She stayed in bed after sunrise, when she usually got up, and indulged herself with memories. She felt warmth and melancholy together, thinking about her mother and father, about her brothers and sisters, all dead. She remembered previous birthdays, parties, special outings, small gifts now lost. The sun moved half an hour closer to noon while Irene lay in bed. She heard her great-nephew and his family moving about in the other rooms of the house. Still she did not get up. Her thin arms rested on the old quilt, her mottled hands folded together over her chest. She felt her lower lip quiver, and she had a recurring twitch in her left cheek. That made her feel old. She didn't like that feeling; she shook her head slightly, as if to shake the growing feeling of depression from her mind.

A bird began to sing in one of the trees near her window. Irene listened. "The bird is awake and about," she said to herself. "It's time for me, too." She pulled back the covers slowly, swung her legs over the edge of the bed, and sat up. She put her feet into her old comfortable slippers and stood up. She put on a frayed robe over her nightgown, tied the belt in a loose knot, and made up her bed. The bird in the yard sang again. Irene clucked her tongue and walked slowly to her door. "It's my birthday, bird," she murmured. "I'm eighty-two years old today. In eighty-two years, I haven't done as much as you have. You have baby chicks, don't you, bird? In eighty-two years, I haven't found the time for children." Irene opened the door and went out into the long, high-ceilinged hallway. She walked silently toward the family dining room. She wondered if her great-nephew would remember that it was her birthday.

Michael, his wife, Constance, and their daughter, Alyse lived in an immense house in what had once been downtown Louisville. All traces of the city had been obliterated, and dense forest covered the whole area. It had been that way for centuries. No one in the world had ever seen a city. References to cities and their problems were common in materials left over from the old times, but they were difficult to comprehend. To Irene, to Michael and his family, cities were like dinosaurs; they certainly had ruled the world at one time, but they were almost impossible to accept emotionally. There were so few people now, so few settlements. The world had gone back to unspoiled nature and no one wanted to change it. The last men of the old times, the last industrialists, the last scientists, the last administrators and executives, the last paid laborers, had all worked with their last resources to destroy nearly every trace that they had existed. They removed the marks that man had made on his world. It was a project that consumed decades, scores of them, along with millions of lives, along with the accumulated wealth and knowledge and skills of the entire race.

The world was changed. It was changed into what the people of the old times thought was a better world. It was greener now, it was lovelier, it was fresher, there were more birds, animals, and flowers. There was no crowding, no pollution of air and water, no noise, no racial tensions, no hunger. Now there was no one to decide if it was better. There was no one who could compare. Irene, in her ignorance of what life in the old times had been like, hoped that the old people had known what they were doing. It was too late to change back.

Her Great-nephew Michael had inherited the huge old house from his father. Michael was only thirty-four years old, but he was the master of a domain some 250 miles square. Michael's parents were living in another large house, near what had once been West Virginia. That house had always been a vacation home, but Michael's mother preferred it. Michael had been given the great house as a wedding present, along with the responsibility of caring for Great-aunt Irene.

Irene sometimes thought of herself as a kind of legacy, to be passed from family member to family member. She didn't mind. The family loved her, and Michael and Constance had the most comfortable home and the fewest burdens. Irene thought of herself as a roll of one-five-four in a game of gabrio. Not as bad as a three-three-seven, not as good as a one-one-one. To her relatives, she was about equal to burning one's tongue on a spoonful of very good but very hot soup. Not pleasant, but not fatal.

The sun shone in through the windows as she walked along the hallway. The wood paneling glowed in bright rectangles. Irene could see golden motes of dust swarming in the sunlight. She walked through the warm clouds and disturbed them. As she got closer to the dining room she heard laughter. It was Constance, laughing at something her husband had said. Their daughter, Alyse, was fifteen years old; she was Irene's great-great-niece. That thought made Irene pause for a moment. She had a great-great-niece, so Irene must be very old. She was eighty-two.

Irene raised one hand slowly to her lips. She was very old. Then she made an impatient gesture. "So what?" she said aloud. She walked on toward the dining room. The sounds of laughter came again. Irene wondered if they were getting ready a surprise for her birthday.

"Good morning, Aunt Irene," said Constance, a few moments later.

"Good morning, dear," said Irene. Her voice sounded strangely harsh to her.

"Did you sleep well?" asked Michael, coming toward the table and carrying a small cage covered with a white cloth. Irene nodded, looking at the cage. Michael removed the cloth. There was a little white animal in the cage.

"What is it, Michael?" asked Alyse.

"It's a baby cat," her father told her. "I caught it by the well."

"It's a kitten," said Irene.

"Yes," said Michael, "that's what they call it."

"What are you going to do with it?" asked Constance. She looked at the kitten and shuddered.

Michael put the cage down on the table and sat at his place. "I thought of hanging it in the sunroom."

"Not in my clean house you won't," said Constance. "And get it off the table. We're going to eat breakfast here. That thing's filthy. Who knows what kind of disease it's carrying?"

Irene sat down in her chair, sighing a little. She folded her hands in her lap. "They're very clean animals, as I recall," she said.

"It won't be any problem," said Michael.

"Can we keep it, Constance?" asked Alyse.

Her mother shook her head. "No," she said, "definitely not. I won't have it in the house."

"Oh, please?" said Alyse. "I'll take care of it."

"No, not in the house. Either let it go or keep it in the barn."

Michael stood up. "All right, Constance," he said. "I'll put it in the barn. It'll be fine out there."

"We could let it loose in the barn," said Alyse. "It could run and play. I could teach it to do tricks."

"Not kittens," said Constance. "They are mean, vicious animals. You can't tame them. They grow up to be killers."

"That little thing?" asked Alyse. "It couldn't hurt anything."

"I've heard stories, Alyse," said Constance. "They grow up and turn on their masters. That's why you have to keep them in cages.

They eat meat, like we do. One day that kitten will be a cat. Then it won't think anything of slashing you and eating you."

"That's just a plain house cat," said Michael. "You're thinking of lions. *They* get big and dangerous. This kitten won't ever get much bigger than a rabbit. It's harmless."

"I don't believe it," said Constance. "My father told me all about them."

"Ask Aunt Irene," said Michael.

"Oh," said Alyse, "she won't help. She's so old, she doesn't remember anything anymore."

"Alyse!" said Michael. "Don't you ever talk like that about anyone! Apologize to Aunt Irene."

"It's true," said Alyse sullenly. "She's always saying things to keep me from having what I want."

Irene felt her face flushing. "I just say what I know," she said.

"That's not much, these days," said Alyse.

"That's enough," said Constance. "Go to your rooms and stay there."

"But today's the party at Felicia's house," said Alyse. "I have to go over there after breakfast and help with the decorations."

"You'll just have to miss it," said Michael. "Now go to your rooms."

"See?" said Alyse, as she stood up from the table. "See? It's all Aunt Irene's fault again. If it weren't for her, everything would be fine. She's so old. She's always getting me in trouble. She's always making me miss things."

Irene felt tears in her eyes. She raised one hand and wiped the tears away. "Constance," she said, "let her stay. Let her go to her party. I know how it is with her. She just doesn't understand."

Constance's expression was stern. "She'll have to learn, that's all."

"See?" said Alyse. "She's doing it again. She's making you hate me."

"Alyse, go to your rooms. Right now," said Michael.

"Let her stay, dear," said Irene. There was a long silence. Irene was very embarrassed. Alyse watched her mother. Michael looked at his great-aunt.

"All right," said Constance at last. "You may go to the party if you apologize to Aunt Irene."

"I apologize," said Alyse in a voice hardly above a whisper.

"Thank you, dear," said Irene.

"All right," said Michael, "let's eat breakfast."

"Put that animal in the barn first," said Constance. Her husband nodded but did not say anything. He carried the cage out of the room.

Irene took a deep breath and sat back in her chair. Her expression did not show the emotions she felt inside. She had taught herself at an early age to keep her feelings to herself. She wondered sometimes if that was a wise thing to do. She was certain that Michael, Constance, and Alyse believed that she was a little cold, a little distant. Perhaps they thought that Aunt Irene had become slightly senile, out of touch with her surroundings, unaffected by events, all because she rarely showed joy, sorrow, or anger. Irene knew better, of course; she knew how deeply Alyse's words had hurt, how happy she felt looking at the kitten, how sad the cage around the kitten had made her. The only outward sign of these feelings had been the quickly wiped-away tears. She knew how the kitten felt. Irene was caged in the house. She was caged in her body. She was caged by the weariness of eighty-two years.

Alyse wouldn't understand that. Alyse was sixty-seven years younger than Irene. Sixty-seven years! thought Irene. Much more than a half century. There were too many generations between them. It was impossible for Irene to teach anything to Alyse; it was just as impossible for the young girl to say anything to the old woman. Irene looked across the table at her great-great-niece. Alyse was impatiently toying with her silverware, waiting for the servants to bring breakfast. Irene knew that whatever Alyse learned about life, she would have to learn the hard way. There was no way for one generation to pass experience on to the next. That was the main cause of grief and the primary source of pleasure in life.

"I hung the kitten up between Blaze's stall and Lucky's," said Michael. His words roused Irene from her thoughts. Michael pulled out his chair and sat down.

Constance smiled. "That's fine, Michael. I just didn't want a wild animal in the house. You know how they make me feel. Sometimes I just can't breathe."

"When are we going to eat?" asked Alyse.

"Yes," said Michael, "Cook should be finished. Why don't you call for Man?"

Constance picked up a small wooden mallet and hit a small brass gong on the table in front of her. A moment later a middle-aged man came into the family dining room. He was dressed in black coat and trousers, white vest, white shirt, and black scarf. He wore a gold chain from his vest, with a great many keys hanging from it. He stopped just inside the doorway, his expression serious, looking at the far wall of the room. He never looked at any of the family members seated at the table, even when he was addressed. He had been with Michael's family, and his parents, and with his father's parents; nonetheless, he still appeared to be slightly past forty years old. No one knew how old Man was, not even Aunt Irene.

"Good morning, Man," said Constance.

"Good Morning, madame," said Man. He stared above her head. In all the years that the family had known Man, they had never seen him look directly at another person.

"We wish to be served breakfast now, if you will."

"Yes, madame." Man turned around and left the dining room. He did not make a sound as he walked away.

"Tell me, Michael," said Constance, "what have you planned for today?"

Michael bit a fingernail as he thought. "I'm not certain yet, Constance," he said. "I have two or three things to decide among. We might travel to one of the meadows and observe the flowers. We might lie upon some hill and attempt to find shapes in cloud formations. We haven't done that since last fall. Or, again, we might retire to the third-floor right front parlor to sing songs, while you or I play one of the musical instruments. We might try to start a garden, with blooming plants or vegetables, near the house or at some distance. We might find some creek or river and pass the day skipping stones and smiling. Or we might—"

"Oh, Michael," said Constance, "our lives are so full!"

"Yes, my dear," he said. "We have so much for which to be grateful."

"I am, Michael," she said. "I thank my private ghosts every night and every morning for the wonderful miracle of our life together."

Michael reached out and took one of Constance's hands in his. "I do the same," he said. "Every night and every morning. Just the way they did it in the old books."

The two adults looked at each other. There was a pleasant stillness for a while, until it was interrupted by Alyse. "I want to get some stamps," she said.

"Stamps?" asked Constance. "What are stamps?"

"They are things that people collect," said Alyse.

"Oh," said her mother, "I must have some of them, then."

Alyse was excited. "You do? Oh, Constance, what do they look like? What color are they? Where are they from?"

Constance only laughed quietly. "The impatience of youth," she said. "Aunt Irene, Alyse probably seems so intense to you."

Irene turned to look at Alyse. The girl, obviously embarrassed, stared at the table. "I am gladdened by her," said Irene.

At that moment Man re-entered the dining room, pushing a cart laden with bowls, platters, and pitchers, filled with the day's breakfast foods. "You may serve us now, Man," said Michael.

"Yes, master," said Man. Behind him walked Woman, dressed in a long white dress with a black bow around her neck. She wore a white cap, with her long black hair in a braid down her back. Man stopped the cart near the table and stood aside. Woman served Constance first, then Michael, then Irene, and finally Alyse. When she finished, Woman stepped away from the table. Together, silently, Man and Woman backed away. They turned and went out of the family dining room.

"Do you know what stamps are, Aunt Irene?" asked Constance.

"No," said Alyse, "she's too busy being gladdened."

"Alyse," said Michael.

"It's all right, Michael," said Irene. She turned to Constance. "I've read of stamps, of course. If Alyse is collecting them, I would be very interested in seeing them. I have never witnessed one before."

"You don't witness a stamp," said Alyse scornfully. "You don't witness them. You lick them."

"Lick them?" asked Michael.

"That's what you do, Michael," said Alyse. "You lick them and put them on things. I want to collect them."

"What do you put them on?" said Constance.

"Letters," said Alyse. "I don't know exactly what they are. I don't care, though. Let someone else collect the letters. I'm just collecting stamps."

"How many do you have, my dear?" asked Irene.

"See?" said Alyse. "See how stupid? I don't have any, as if you didn't know. There aren't any stamps anymore. If *you* haven't ever seen one, what makes you think I have?"

Irene said nothing. When she was hurt the most she said nothing.

"Alyse," said Michael, "I don't like the way you've been speaking to Aunt Irene. I want you to apologize."

Alyse spoke through gritted teeth. "I apologize."

Irene said nothing.

"This is good," said Constance, trying to change the subject, trying to relieve the tension in the room.

"Yes," said Michael, "the breakfast is good."

"Our Cook is remarkable," said Irene. "I have never enjoyed meals quite so much. Every day is like a festive occasion. I always take delight in the pleasant garnishes and the attractive colors, fragrances, and flavors. Cook is a treasure."

"Don't forget to include Man and Woman," said Constance.

"Of course," said Irene. "Man and Woman are indeed treasures, also."

"Yes," said Constance.

There was a lull in the table talk, while the four people ate their breakfast. Irene noticed that Alyse frequently stared at her, and the look in the young girl's eyes was unpleasant, even threatening.

Man and Woman returned, just as everyone finished the morning meal. They took away the bowls and platters and pitchers. When the family was alone again in the dining room, Constance turned to her daughter. "Why do you want to collect stamps, my dear, when you've never seen one? You aren't likely to come across one, you know. You're asking for frustration and disappointment. Why did you choose stamps?"

"Because," said Alyse.

Michael laughed. "Yes, yes," he said. "I remember that reason very well. That is the most persuasive argument a young person has. 'Because.' What humiliating failures are suffered on its account."

"I will not be humiliated," said Alyse. "Not by a stamp. I *hate* being humiliated."

"We all do, dear," said Constance.

Alyse stared at Irene. "Some people must not," she said slowly, "judging by the number of times they are humiliated. Some people must enjoy it, they do it so often."

"Alyse," said Michael. The girl ignored her father.

"How are you feeling today, Aunt Irene?" asked Constance.

"I am very well today," said Irene.

"That's good," said Michael. "Are your eyes better?"

Irene took a deep breath and sighed again. "I am old," she said. "I am eighty-two years old. My eyes will not get better."

Constance dabbed at the corners of her mouth with her napkin. "Have you thought about improving your eyesight with eyeglasses?"

"I have," said Irene. "I have also thought about improving my hearing with a mechanical aid, my heart with an electronic device, my legs with braces, my few remaining teeth with dentures, my feet with special shoes, my palsy, arthritis, neuralgia, and indigestion with chemical aids and exotic treatments. But I have too many failures of flesh, too many breakdowns in my body, too many ailments, infirmities, disorders, attacks, mild convulsions, fevers, swellings, inflammations, and infections to overcome. I feel lost. The cycles of disease are too strong to break. The worn-out members and organs are too closely related. I cannot conquer them before they co-operate to conquer me."

"That's a horrible way to talk, Aunt Irene," said Constance. "It frightens me to listen. You make life sound so hopeless, so ugly. If all that is true, what can you do about it?"

"You can't do anything about it," said Irene. "You can only count your blessings."

"Count your blessings!" cried Alyse. "How many do you have?"

"These days, I count five," said Irene.

"If you spent more time counting your five blessings," said Alyse, "and less time—"

"Alyse," said Constance, "go to your rooms. Now. And don't come down until you're ready to apologize to Aunt Irene."

"But Constance, I—"

"You heard me. Now go."

Alyse glared at her mother, then turned to Irene. "All right," she muttered, "I apologize."

"No good," said Michael.

"I apologized," said Alyse.

Constance shook her head. "Go to your rooms and stay there until Woman calls you for luncheon. We'll see if you've learned a little pity for Aunt Irene then."

Pity! thought Irene. She showed a small bit of her distaste, but no one was looking. As quickly as it had come the expression changed again, to her normal, placid appearance. She didn't have the slightest desire for anyone's pity. That was the one thing, in fact, that she hated most about her old age. She could count on the love of Michael and Constance, but it was the kind of love that people gave to animals and objects that have been kept for long periods of time. It was only familiarity, love by default. She never had anyone's respect. Instead, she received tokens of sympathy, compassion—and pity. People had a tendency to overlook her errors or accidents too quickly, in recognition of her age and the accompanying decrepitude they believed must exist. Irene resented that; she could never again win the regard that her mind and achievements justified. Honest love, true respect, natural courtesy: All these had ended at some arbitrary point somewhere in her past.

Alyse glared again at Irene, and again at Constance. Alyse turned and went angrily to the entrance of the dining room. She almost knocked into Man, who was coming in. She glared at him, also.

"What is it, Man?" asked Michael.

"I wish to know if master or madame would like today's rain this morning, or later in the afternoon," said Man. He stood politely three steps into the dining room, his hands clasped behind his back, his posture stiff and straight.

"Do you have any preference, dear?" asked Constance.

"Yes," said Michael. "I was thinking of going hunting after luncheon. I'd rather not have it raining then."

"Shall I arrange for the rain before luncheon, master?" asked Man.

"Just a moment, please. Constance, what do you want to do today?"

Constance's brows drew closer together as she thought. "I hate days like this," she said. "I don't like it when there's a whole day with nothing in it, and we have to find ways of spending the time. Are you sure there aren't any emergencies planned for this morning? No accidents, no freaks of nature, that kind of thing?"

"I am quite certain, madame," said Man.

"I hate it," said Constance. "I don't know. What about this morning, Michael? Pick something. Anything. Just to get it over with."

Michael thought for a moment. He rubbed his forehead and then looked at his wife. "Well," he said at last, "we'll ride out to one of the lodges, check its stores, and build a grove. Or a lake, if there already is a grove."

"Fine," said Constance, smiling. "I'm glad you thought of something. We haven't done that in such a long time."

"Do you understand, Man?" asked Michael.

"Yes, sir. The rain will end at eleven o'clock. You will then have enough time to return, refresh yourselves, and change clothes for luncheon."

"Excellent, Man," said Constance. "We can watch the rain from the lodge. We can play games with it, just like when we were younger. I think this day will be a lot of fun, better than I thought it would be. It's going to be a special day."

Michael laughed. "Yes, Constance, it's a special day, and for a special reason that you've probably forgotten."

Irene allowed herself a brief, small smile. Michael hadn't forgotten his aunt's birthday, after all.

"What do you mean, dear?" asked Constance.

"I mean that with Alyse in her rooms, we'll be at liberty to try some more experimentation."

"Do you mean love-making, Michael?" asked Constance. "I thought we'd exhausted that, oh, long ago."

"Didn't you enjoy it?"

"Certainly," said Constance, "but I thought you meant something new."

Irene was disappointed. She sighed. She folded her hands in her lap. Her hands shook. She watched them. They were discolored; the skin was yellowish and there were large brown spots. She hadn't had those spots when she was Constance's age. She tried to recall when they had first appeared. She couldn't remember.

"There isn't much that's new," said Michael. "There's not much to choose from. We have to make the best of what we have."

Constance rubbed her eyes with one hand. "Oh, Michael, sometimes I'm so tired. It's so hard to keep going, to keep thinking of new ways to spend the time."

Irene thought about Constance's words. Constance was only thirty-one years old. Nevertheless, Constance seemed already worn out by living. Irene enjoyed life, even the meager life that an old person is permitted among the young. Irene would have loved to go with them to the lodge, to build a grove or lake as she did when she was a girl. But neither Constance nor Michael would have allowed it, if she had made the suggestion.

"It's not so bad, Constance," said Michael. "Just leave that all to me. That's my job."

"Then what is my job to be?" asked his wife.

Michael was silent for a moment. "The same as always," he said at last. "Whatever you want it to be."

"Oh, Michael, that isn't an answer. That just makes it all worse."

"I'm sorry, then," he said. "I love you, Constance."

"I love you, Michael."

The two rose from their seats. Michael came around the table and took Constance's hand. They walked out of the room together, chatting in low tones. Irene couldn't hear their words. As they left the dining room, Man looked toward Irene. She shook her head and waved one hand slightly. Man nodded and followed behind Michael and Constance. Irene was left alone at the table.

She felt discontent. She felt forgotten, abandoned, futile. She felt like an atrophied organ in the body of the family, a useless appendage, a vestigial remnant of something that had once been meaningful and important. Her head began to ache. She massaged her temples. She felt her pulse beating strongly on the side of her head. Sometimes she hated the structures of her body. They were all slowly failing, and she feared that some day when, like now, she was aware of her heartbeat, she would be touching the pulse at the very moment when it stopped forever. She was afraid that her consciousness would last beyond that instant, to make her death one of supreme terror. She would know that she was dead, even as she was fading away. "I'm dead, I'm dead, I'm dead, I'm—"

Irene stopped rubbing her temples and folded her hands in her lap once more. Then she stood up slowly. Her back hurt, and she felt a momentary dizziness. She leaned against the chair until it passed. Then she pushed the chair toward the table and walked out of the dining room. Her own quarters were on the same floor, a thoughtful arrangement that had been suggested by Woman.

It took Irene a few minutes to get to her rooms, because she decided to stop along the way and look out all the windows. She liked mornings. At the age of eighty-two, she had witnessed a great number of them; it was a constant source of wonder to her that each one had been different. She wished that Constance, Michael, and Alyse could understand that.

When she got to her apartments, Irene shut the door and locked it. She passed through her bedroom, through the large dressing room, through the clothes storage room, through the large bath, through the atrium, through her indoor greenhouse, through her library, through the music room, the art room, the sewing room, the small bath, until she arrived at her special, private, secret room. She kept her collection here. She was immensely proud of her collection, but not so proud that she wished to share it with everyone. She kept the collection for her own amusement. She never felt the need to be praised or admired because of the things she had. She wanted to be praised and admired because of all that she was.

One common amusement among the people of Irene's acquaintance was collecting. Everyone wanted to put together pieces of the ancient days, the dark days, the dawn of civilization. Alyse collected stamps, or at least wanted to. Michael collected stones and pieces of metal with words on them. Constance collected pins, needles, nails, screws, bolts, and tacks, all items that had been made useless by progress.

Irene collected glass, a particular, rare kind of glass. While still in her youth, Irene had been given a fiche—a microfilm card that reproduced an entire book in a space five inches by three. The book was a catalog and price list of twentieth-century Depression glass, compiled by a woman named Elizabeth Dawson Douglas. The book was made many years before the Peaceful Revolution. The book fascinated Irene. It described the collecting of glass made during the twentieth-century Depression, which Irene's father said was a medieval time of disruption. The language of the times was odd and unpleasant, to Irene's tastes, but the author wrote of the glassware in such a way that made Irene want to discover some.

The glass had been produced in hundreds and hundreds of patterns, each in several distinct colors, and each pattern consisting of many different pieces. The object, as Irene understood it, was to collect the pattern of one's choice in the color of one's choice, and collect each individual piece, checking against the list on the fiche. The early savages had collected the glass, which was already somewhat rare in Mrs. Douglas' time. Completing a set was an exciting accomplishment, even then. Irene felt a kind of kinship with her predecessors by searching for the same objects.

After nearly seventy years of collecting, Irene owned twelve pieces that she could absolutely identify as twentieth-century Depression glass. She had three pieces that were not definitely catalogued in the fiche but that looked as though they might belong to the same period. Irene knew that she might never know the truth about them. She felt that she had the best collection of twentieth-century Depression glass in the modern world. She had never heard of anyone else who had even a single piece.

Irene opened the cabinet in which she kept her collection. The bright sunlight beamed and sparkled on the fifteen pieces of glass. Irene smiled. She felt peaceful for the first time since waking up that morning. She took out each piece, just as she did every morning. She held each piece up to the light. The glass was beautiful. It was rare. The fifteen pieces were one of Irene's five blessings.

Four of the pieces were the same color, in the same pattern. They were a light, transparent green. The pattern, according to the authoritative catalogue of Mrs. Douglas, was called Doric. It was very lovely in a simple, uncluttered way. Irene had a dinner plate, a cup, a sherbet dish, and a covered butter dish.

She had a green Sunflower cake plate.

Two pieces of glass were uncolored crystal. One was from a pattern called Bubble; it was a cereal bowl. The other was a pitcher from the Iris pattern.

Four pieces of glass were pink. One belonged to a pattern called

Lace Edge, a cookie jar with its lid missing. Two were of a pattern called Miss America; one was a divided grill plate and the other was a relish dish. A fourth pink piece was a platter of the Princess pattern.

The last piece that Irene could identify was amber in color. It was a Patrician creamer.

Along with these were a milk-white citrus reamer, a blue mug with a picture of a young girl that was signed "Shirley Temple," and a green candleholder in the shape of a dolphin.

These were Irene's treasures. They were an important part of her life, and they had helped to keep her alive. The search had kept her going for seventy years. While she looked at her precious collections, she felt strong and young enough to search for another twenty years.

Chapter Two

An Old Woman's Broken Heart

At nine o'clock, just as Irene was locking her glass back in the cabinet, there was a light tapping on the door. Irene sighed. The same knock came every morning. Irene dreaded it.

"Come in," she called,

"I'm sorry, madame," came Woman's voice from the other side of the door, "but it's locked."

"Oh," said Irene, pretending to be surprised. She pretended to be surprised every morning. "I'm sorry, Woman. Just a moment." Irene moved her hands over her robe, vainly trying to straighten the ancient wrinkles in the material. She turned the lock on the door and waited for Woman to come into the room.

"Time for our little bath," said Woman. Irene shuddered a little. "It's a beautiful morning," said Woman.

"Yes," said Irene. She followed as Woman turned and walked toward the large bath.

"How are you feeling this morning?" asked Woman. "Do you need any help?" She didn't turn around when she spoke. Irene followed in her path like a duckling.

"I'm fine," she said. "I don't need any help at all. I don't even need any help taking a bath. I'm really fine."

"That's good," said Woman. "Still, it's a good idea to let me help. We wouldn't want any accidents."

There hadn't been any accidents in a long time. Irene was very proud of her good safety record. But that didn't mean a thing to her family and the servants. The fact that Irene hadn't had a serious injury meant only that it was likely that she *would*, sooner or later. Her number was coming up. Woman had to be on her guard, especially in the bath. Michael had given Woman particular instructions about the bath. The location of the soap had to be known at every moment. Old people often slipped on soap. Woman was at attention at all critical times. Irene wished that if she were going to have an accident, she could arrange to have one at an uncritical moment, when Woman's close scrutiny was relaxed a bit. Irene wondered if she could hurt herself with a towel.

"Well, here we are in the large bath," said Woman, in case Irene hadn't recognized the room.

"Do yon have your own bath?" asked Irene.

"Yes," said Woman. "It's very nice, but not as nice as yours."

"Is your bath as nice as Man's?"

Woman turned and stared for several seconds. "I don't know," she said finally, her voice a shade cooler. "I've never had occasion to see Man's bath."

"I didn't mean anything by it," said Irene. She was happy. She had had an affect on Woman. Irene was still a force to be reckoned with. "I'm sorry if I offended you."

"Not at all," said Woman. She was already filling the tub. Irene wondered if Woman would seek reprisal through water temperature. She dismissed the thought; it: was unworthy, just as mean and crotchety as Alyse had said Irene was. That made her feel unpleasant. Possibly it. meant that she had already gone to the point where her visions of the world were inaccurate, that she had really become senile and not known it, that she was having a transitory moment of lucidity in an otherwise horrifying and loathsome existence. Irene thought about that as she lowered herself, with Woman's constant aid, into the bathtub. "Woman," she said, "am I a problem to you?"

"No, not at all," said Woman. The tone of her voice conveyed nothing, not a hint of emotion.

"Do I embarrass you or the others, sometimes? Do I drool and lose control of my bodily functions? Do I ramble on and on about the most absurd things, or forget where I am and talk to people long dead? Have I lost my mental faculties?"

Woman was soaping a large sponge, which was a pleasant shade of light blue to match the light-blue tiles set at random among the gleaming white tiles of the bathroom. She stopped momentarily, holding the soap in one hand, the sponge in the other. "No, madame," said Woman, "as long as I can recall, you've been almost exactly the same. You've never embarrassed yourself, either in word or deed."

Irene smiled. She let herself slip a little more beneath the warm water. It felt very good. She still didn't know if Woman were telling the truth, but there was no way she could test the servant. The only plan might be to question Man and get his answer, and ask Michael, Constance, and then Alyse, all separately. In this way she could arrive at a consensus, and she could decide for herself whether or not she had become senile, or if she were merely old, highly numbered in years but still vigorous, perceptive, and fully sane.

Woman began washing Irene, and the old woman moved slowly in the warm water, just as she did every day. She extended one arm and Woman soaped it. Irene extended the other arm, and it was washed. Then Woman washed Irene's neck and back, then her chest. Woman worked efficiently and silently. Irene's movements came from habit, but her thoughts were elsewhere. She knew that her opinion of herself had been damaged somewhat by Alyse, and by the attitudes of the others in the house. She didn't like that. She didn't like being intimidated into self-pity. She didn't know what she could do about it, but she had the confidence that she would find the answer if she put her mind, her intelligence, and her experience to work.

"There we are," said Woman. "All clean. Now, madame, if you will stand up."

Irene stood up. At that instant she knew what she had to do. She had to continue the motion ordered by Woman. She stood up and was toweled dry by Woman, and she put on her robe. Woman guided her back to her chambers and left. Irene was alone. She went straight to her principal bureau and began packing a small case with essential articles of clothing and cosmetics. She was going to leave the house. She had lived in the house all her life, but now she knew that it offered her nothing as she grew older. She might die in the house and be buried with a minimum of sadness, out on the far hill where the other relatives were buried, but there would never be a moment of joy or sorrow—either would be welcome, as a change—as long as she stayed in the house. She would have to seek these things elsewhere. The idea, the concept of *elsewhere* made her feel uncomfortable, and that alone persuaded her that her decision was correct. She had to run away.

Beside the small case, Irene packed a basket of fruit and sandwiches to eat along the way. She didn't have any specific plans, but that was part of the excitement. Suddenly the future looked troublesome. She exulted in the mood. She encouraged it. The future looked difficult, and that was a symbol, a sign that she was still alive, still able to face problems. It didn't mean that she could actually solve those problems, but she wasn't seeking security. At home, here with Michael and Constance, she had more security than she could tolerate. The future might be desperate, and that would give her pleasure, more pleasure than the daily routines in the house. She might even meet true danger—her very *life* might be threatened! Irene shuddered. In that case, she thought, she would be saved by her wits and skills, or she would die. And then, once more, she would gratefully accept either outcome. At the very least, she wouldn't have to be carried out to the hill and planted next to the other members of the family, some of whom she had never met, others whom she despised, and all of whom were too tedious in life to have to spend eternity next to. She would definitely prefer her death in the jungles of the outer world, ripped by claws, crushed by mighty animal limbs, torn by slavering fangs, killed by the laws of the natural world, where she could serve some purpose in her last act, where she could provide nourishment to the predatory creatures she had rarely before imagined. Her grave would be empty, her flesh eaten and not defiled by mere decay, her bones left to mingle with the soil and, all in all, she thought as she carried her packages from the room, a delightful and spiritual way to say good-bye to a world that had never troubled her very much in her eight decades of tenancy.

No one saw her as she left the house; she didn't want to be seen, and she had known since childhood how to move without drawing attention. She followed the gravel driveway out to the road. Then came her first decision: left or right? In either direction were long distances of forest, the dirt road the only sign that human beings had intruded. The nearest neighbors were twelve miles to the left, and fifteen miles to the right. She chose the latter.

After a while the road grew narrower until it stopped being a road and began being a ratted path through grass and weeds. Irene was tired. She had hobbled slowly for nearly an hour, and she decided that she had to sit and rest. She sat in the shade of a large tree and opened the basket of sandwiches. She ate one, delighting in the feeling of independence. The sandwich made her thirsty. She suddenly realized that she had forgotten to bring anything to drink. That was a sure sign that she was getting incompetent, she thought. Alyse would have laughed. Irene ate an apple, and the juice of the fruit quenched her thirst. She packed everything again and began walking.

Not long after that she noticed that the sky was covering over with black clouds. "Rain," muttered Irene. "I forgot that, too. Man was going to make rain before lunchtime." The thunderheads piled up threateningly. Lightning cracked the darkness, stabbing down like sabers at the earth. Thunder rolled in the distance, then rambled closer, then exploded as though directly overhead. The rain came down so heavily that Irene was soaked before she could find shelter. She was cold and wet and completely miserable. The two pieces of her baggage were suddenly very heavy, and Irene wished that she could throw them away, but she knew that if she were really running away she would need them. "I've been treated like a pet fish in that house," she thought. "They give me a little care, but they're ready to flush me down the toilet at any time." She was determined to leave Michael and Constance forever, but as the rain came down harder her will began to dissolve. "Man surely knows how to make a storm," she thought.

Irene had received an invitation. She didn't understand where the invitation had come from, but it was a definite offer to leave the house and discover the world. She had accepted at first, because of simple curiosity and more than a little boredom and a bit of offended pride. Irene saw her life as a rich source of information and advice. She had answers, but she knew that the rest of the family refused her knowledge, possibly for fear of "contamination" with her old age. Irene knew that without her answers the family would lose more and more of its treasured heritage. She had tried to explain, but they never listened. But now, as the storm and darkness increased, she changed her mind. She didn't want to give up what she now saw as her own best interest. Life in Michael's house, under whatever circumstances, was preferable to the wild roaming existence and death she foresaw as the result of her sudden running away. Regretfully she refused the invitation. She carried her two pieces of baggage and trudged back toward the house, along the grassy lane that was now ankle-deep in mud. The rain came down for exactly fifteen minutes until Man stopped it, and by that time Irene was so unhappy and discouraged that she hardly had the persistence to keep walking. Only the thought of the humiliating death that would be hers if she fell to the ground here, in the mud, not far from the house, kept her going. She would go back to the house, back to her apartments, back to her few pieces of glass and the unbearable attitudes of the others.

"There were things that happened when I was young," she thought, "and I can't remember why, but they caused everyone great happiness. Holidays, special times, things that I've forgotten. These things are gone forever. There are other things that I've told Michael and Constance, but they're too busy to remember. These, too, will be forgotten. When I'm gone, there will be only a poor parody of life in that house." She walked on, and the grassy path became a muddy road. She was not far from the house. "They just want to let me be, undisturbed until I die. How kind they are." Irene made a face as though she had bitten into a piece of rotten fruit. She spat. "I've been shut off in my rooms," she thought. "Segregated, left apart like a person of the wrong religion or wrong race or wrong politics or wrong infirmity. For them, my old age is more frightening than death itself."

She saw the house and wanted to get back to her rooms without being seen by anyone. She looked terrible, she knew, all soaking wet and straggly-haired, carrying the small bag of clothing and the basket of food, and she didn't want to have to answer any questions. She slipped back into the house and hurried to her rooms. She threw the bag and basket into her bedroom and went into the large bathroom to take a warm shower. She let the warm water pour down over her body, taking away the chill of the rainstorm and the slow journey home. She dried herself off, put on a robe, and went back to the bedchamber. She heard sounds from her innermost room. She hurried through the rooms in fear. When she got there, she had the most unpleasant surprise of her eighty-two years.

"Hello, Aunt Irene," said Alvse. The girl was sitting in one of the wing chairs in the chamber, looking through a pile of Irene's clothing.

"You've taken my clothing out of the bureau and dresser," said Irene. "You earned it into this room. Why? Would you like me to show you something?"

Alyse laughed. "I was just bored. I mean, someone as old as you doesn't need much in the way of clothing, do you? What for? Clothing is supposed to be attractive, like a magnet is attractive. Do you think that if you wear these things, you will be attractive? Whom would you attract? Or what, if that's the proper word. Do you think this underwear, these hose, this dress, will cause males to flock about you helplessly, against their will, hopelessly attracted?"

"That is not the only purpose of clothing," said Irene. She took the clothes and started carrying them back to their places.

"No," said Alyse, "I suppose not. They can be used to keep warm. And to hide the incredible ugliness of one's body."

Irene didn't answer, but she winced at the insult.

"I don't understand how you can stand to stay in this house," said Alyse. "No one wants you here. You know that, don't you?"

"It's something that I've known for years," said Irene. "It's not altogether true, but I realize that sometimes I'm resented. Even Man and Woman act as if I interfere. Sometimes."

"Don't worry," said Alyse carelessly, "you'll be dead soon."

"Yes," said Irene. She stared out the window, as the rain had stopped and the clouds had all gone away, just as Man had been instructed. There was a beautiful rainbow visible through the window. Irene took a deep breath of the fresh, rain-washed air. "There's a rainbow," she said softly.

"Michael's hunting this afternoon," said Alyse. "Killing things."

"So I understand."

"Constance is in her apartments, working on her tapestry," said the girl. "There is no way for her to hear anything, that far away. We'd have to send Man or Woman to get her, if we needed her."

"Do we need her?" asked Irene. "Will we?"

"No," said Alyse. "I guess not."

Irene selected the clothing she would wear that afternoon. She thought back over the last couple of hours, over her abruptly ended attempt at escape. How poor in spirit she must be, if fifteen minutes of Man's rain was enough to destroy her resolve. She wondered what that said about her character. Someone who was an expert in psychology, a field of interest that had become extinct early in Irene's third decade, would have said that she had regressed to an earlier stage, or that she had become fixated at that stage. She was an eighty-two-year-old infant She had become bounded by the walls of a new childhood. Michael's house was, in a way, a new womb, a new cradle, a new nursery. Michael and Constance, as parental figures, guarded the threshold, making her fearful of entering the world.

"We're all alone here," said Alyse.

"Yes, dear," said Irene. She wanted to take the clothing to the dressing room and put on the afternoon's attire, but she had to wait until Alyse left. "Is there something I can help you with? Is there something you'd like to see?"

"Yes, oh yes, Aunt Irene," she said. Irene didn't notice the tone of Alyse's voice, or the look on her face.

Irene was thinking of her own situation. She had been asleep for many years, too many years. She was the Sleeping Beauty, Snow White, Brunhilda, and it would take a special Prince to awaken her. Irene had no doubt that the special Prince would come eventually. She had been expecting him for many years. The special Prince was Death.

"Aunt Irene?" asked Alyse.

"What?" The old woman was embarrassed to be caught daydreaming, as though she were truly a bit crazy and a little stricken in years.

"I'd like to see your collection. I want to have a collection, too, you know. Stamps. But I'd like to see your collection. I want to see how a collection is kept. I want to see how to start, and what to do with the damn things once I've got them."

"Ah," said Irene, smiling. Her glass gave her pleasure, and showing the pieces to others gave her even more pleasure. The glass and the cabinet that housed it, as well as everything else in her apartments, were dustless, absolutely neat and clean. The air in the rooms smelled almost antiseptic, unlike the somewhat decaying aspect of some other parts of the huge house. No surface, no area of the furniture, the windowsills, the moldings along the walls, nowhere was there a trace of dirt. Woman was supposed to be in charge of cleaning, but when Woman finished, Irene went along and removed the dust and dirt that Woman overlooked.

"I've seen the glass before, of course," said Alyse solemnly, "but I'd love, I'd dearly love to see it all again, and have you tell me what it all is, and where you got it, and how valuable it all is."

Irene smiled and went to the cabinet. Next to the cabinet was a wooden stand, darkly stained, on which rested a Bible. The book was usually closed, but Irene noticed that it had been opened by someone or by some trick of wind and draft. The pages were covered with leaves, except for a small portion of one page. Irene read the visible portion, which was from the first book of Proverbs. It said, "Give heed to my reproof; behold, I will pour out my thoughts to you; I will make my words known to you.

"Because I have called and you refused to listen, have stretched out my hand and no one has heeded, and you have ignored all my counsel and would have none of my reproof, I also will laugh at your calamity; I will mock when panic strikes you like a storm, and your calamity comes like a whirlwind, when distress and anguish come upon you."

These words made Irene uneasy. They were the only words visible beneath the leaves that had blown in from the open window. It was the first time that she had read from the Bible in many years. With a worried expression she turned around to look around her room. Everything was in order. There weren't any incipient calamities about, except Alyse, and Irene had known Alyse for years. Irene knew what Alyse was capable of doing, and she also knew that the girl's fear of Michael and Constance would prevent any outright attack. With an impatient gesture Irene swept the leaves to the floor, and closed the Bible on its passage of turning away from the call.

Irene opened the cabinet and took out the Iris pitcher. "Here," she said, "this is called crystal because it is clear, without color."

"It's very beautiful," said Alyse, examining the object. "Do you think collecting stamps could be this exciting?"

"Sure, my dear," said Irene. She felt a wonderful warmth rising in her. She took out the green Sunflower cake plate. "This is something both beautiful and useful," she said. "It is lovely, and very old. It is priceless. There may not be another in the world, that I know of. If Constance wanted, she could bake a cake and we could put it on this plate."

"Constance wouldn't bake a cake," said Alyse. She put the Iris pitcher on the floor, and took the cake plate. "That's what Cook is for, you know. To bake cakes. And she wouldn't put one on that. It's glass. Cook has her own cake plates. They're made out of gold and silver, or something, you know."

"I know," said Irene. She brought out another piece of Depression glass, the covered Doric butter dish. "Be careful with this," she said, "because—"

SMASH.

Alyse had taken the butter dish from Irene clumsily, and the top of the butter dish had fallen off, fallen to the floor, and broken into many, many tiny, sharp, glistening pieces of glass.

There was silence in the room for several seconds. Irene stared at the floor, at the broken lid to her butter dish. Her body felt hot, and her head felt dizzy. She heard her heart beating louder and faster than normal. She looked up and saw Alyse holding the bottom of the butter dish. Alyse was smiling. She was trying not to laugh. "I'm so sorry, Aunt Irene," she said. "I can't tell you how sorry I am."

"You————"

"I'm really sorry," said Alyse. She gave the butter-dish bottom back to Irene, and then the cake plate and the pitcher. Irene felt dream like. She put the glass back in the cabinet and locked it. Then she stood and looked at the hundreds, the thousands of tiny pieces that had been the lid. "Maybe you can get another one," said Alyse.

"No," said Irene.

"Maybe you could fix it."

"No."

There was another long silence. Finally Alyse said, "I'm sorry, Aunt Irene. I'll have to tell Constance about this, and I'll be punished. But that doesn't bother me. I'm so sorry I broke one of your pieces of glass." She was still smiling.

Irene waved her away, and Alyse ran from the room. Irene heard her laughing in the hallway. Irene just stared at the broken glass.

She would leave it there forever, she decided. Her broken Doric butterdish top. Her calamity. Her refusal of the call.

Irene felt anger. It was the first time in years—in decades—that she had known that emotion. She felt rage. She wanted to hurt, she wanted to inflict the actual, physical proof of her fury on Alyse or, failing that, on anyone, anyone at all. She stared around her room, unable to find a satisfactory outlet for her anger. She kicked the shattered green glass around the floor, under her bed, under rugs and furniture. She went to her bed and fell down on it, weeping. After a while she sat up. There was nothing more to be gained by anger. There was no value or point to frustration.

"Well," she thought, "I now own one half of a green Doric butter dish. It is exactly the same situation I would have been in if the green Doric butter dish had had its top missing when I found it years ago. What I would have done then, I must do now. I must find another lid." She took a deep breath. "How do I do that?" she wondered. After a moment of thought she decided to go to her library and take out the microfiche card of the book on twentieth-century Depression glass, the book written by the expert, Mrs. Elizabeth Dawson Douglas. She put the fiche into her reader and examined the book. Mrs. Douglas evidently had had an admirable collection, hundreds and hundreds of pieces in all colors, all patterns, common and very rare pieces all together to marvel at.

"That is where I will find my butter-dish top," thought Irene. "I will go to Mrs. Elizabeth Dawson Douglas' home, I will sort through the remains of her collection, and I will take the piece of glass that I need. While I'm at it, I will take also the crystal Cameo cocktail shaker, as that is extremely rare. And I may also take the cobalt-blue Royal Lace pitcher, for it is very beautiful, and I can give it a better home here than in the deserted, crumbling place that was once the home of Elizabeth Dawson Douglas." Irene looked back to the place that gave information on how to contact Mrs. Douglas. It gave a telephone number. Irene had never heard of a telephone. It gave a post-office box number. Irene had never heard of a post office. It gave a city and a state. Cities had been rumors when Irene was a child, but states had been more like fairy stories. "Springfield, California," thought Irene. "That is where I have to go. Springfield, California. When I get there, I'll just have to ask for directions to Mrs. Douglas' old house."

The distance from Louisville, Kentucky, to Springfield, California, is approximately two thousand, two hundred miles, barring accident, detour, unforeseen events, and topographical details such as the Rocky Mountains. It is a long walk, even for the most athletically inclined and professionally trained young man. For a woman of eighty-two, who had never walked more than five miles at one stretch in her life, it was a curious, one might say foolhardy, decision. Of course, Irene had never heard of California before, and she had no idea how far it was, or even in which direction it was. She lived in the huge house in the never-ending forest, where the city of Louisville had once been. Her decision was made more because of the great loneliness of her old age, a time when she was unable to share; the younger had no interest in her special thoughts, the older were dead. Then, too, she had been rejected by her family, and she had been rejected by the world, in a sense. She had ceased to be a valuable organism, no longer able to reproduce, doing nothing but taking from the environment and replenishing little in return. The final step—rejection by herself— she would never take. This trip to California was the defense she put up against that self-rejection. A project is what she needed, she needed something to focus on, to give her life meaning, a purpose, and a goal. Otherwise she was just an eating and excreting machine, like a ground hog about to die or a mole about to die or a pigeon about to die.

"I will go to California," she said aloud, just as Woman came in with a broom and a dustpan. Irene glanced at her. "The glass?" she asked. Woman nodded. "I've kicked it all over the room. I'm sorry." Woman only nodded.

There was silence in the room while Woman hunted down the last gleaming bit of green glass. "Woman," said Irene after a while, "do you know about California?"

Woman stood up and made a little groaning sound. She put a hand to the small of her back. Irene realized that Woman, too, was beginning to show signs of aging. Both Woman and Man had been in the family for years, decades, who knew how much longer? But were they immortal? Certainly they, too, had to show symptoms of the common bodily failures at some time. Irene felt unsettled; she liked things to stay the same, at least *most* things.

"California?" said Woman. "I heard of California when I was much younger, before I came to this house. I was working in another house, in another part of the forest, many hundreds of miles from here, to the south. The trees were all different, and the birds. But talk of California arose frequently. California is a land of milk and honey and streets paved with gold. California is a land of opportunity, where all men and women may go and find themselves fulfilled as individuals. California is a land where no one, no matter how humble his origins, may stand with head high among equals, and there is enough of everything to go around, and the weather is fair and bright, and the fruit grow the whole year long. Many people have set off in search of California and its infinite treasures, including my two eldest brothers, but no one has ever returned."

"Then how do we know these things about California?" asked Irene.

Woman dropped the pieces of Doric glass into a wastebasket. For a moment in the room there was the musical tinkling of the glass against the metal bottom of the wastebasket. "The fact that no one has returned is proof enough," said Woman. "They have all stayed in California, rather than return to the poverty here and elsewhere."

"All that milk," said Irene.

"All that honey," said Woman.

"And the streets paved with gold, and the clouds with silver."

"A marvelous place," said Woman.

"Then how do we know these things?" asked Irene.

Woman stared at her for a few seconds, chewing her lower lip. "They must be remnants of ancient knowledge," she said at last.

"Ah," said Irene. She liked ancient knowledge.

"There are many wealthy men in California," said Woman. "They are always looking for beautiful and intelligent women to share their lives with, not to mention their honey."

"It must be difficult at night," said Irene, "lonely, walking the fog-shrouded golden streets alone, whistling to keep one's spirits up, seeing the fleeting image of the moon in the glistening, bright golden pavement, then the source of light disappearing again, all, everything, man, moon, gold, in the damp and lonely fog."

"It sounds sad to me," said Woman.

"I will go to them," said Irene. "I will find them and comfort them, and tell them that others wait only for a sign, and they will follow me and end the desolation of the wealthy few in California. And I will find the world's greatest collection of Depression glass."

"Oh," said Woman, "the glass." She sounded disappointed. She had been excited by Irene's talk of the lonely men in California, and the gold, and the milk, and the honey.

"Leave me now," said Irene. "I must plan."

Woman did not reply. She took the broom, the dustpan, and the metal wastebasket and left Irene's apartments.

An hour later Irene had packed a few more things into two lightweight bags, and was ready to leave again. This time, though, she had a goal and a purpose, and that was something that had been missing from her life for many years. It was, she thought, a sixth blessing, and it made all the preparations much simpler. She packed, wrote a note for Michael and Constance telling them not to worry, that she'd be back soon, and if not, well, then they'd be rid of one of their major sources of concern. She said that she loved them all, would miss them all, wished them all good luck, and may God bless them all. She made sure that her rooms were all spotlessly clean and made up as orderly as could be, took a few last, lingering looks around at the things that had made up her life for so many years, sighed a few times, then went outside again. She walked boldly down the drive to the road, turned in the same direction as before, and walked off with the afternoon sun before her. Her instinct told her that California was in that direction. The sun, like the wealthy men, like Irene herself, ended its life in California and was born again every morning behind their backs, to the east. Irene didn't understand how this happened, but she did not question it. She had learned after eighty-two years that there were too many odd things in the world, and that questioning just aggravated the situation.

She followed the road to where it became a grassy trail. She passed the point where she had stopped earlier, and she went on. She hobbled and staggered until she was exhausted. She felt joy and she felt fear, sometimes separately and sometimes mingled. After a while, beside joy and fear, she felt lost. She was lost, farther from home and familiar things than she had ever been before in her life. That was significant. She doubted that she could even find her way home. She followed the sun, which was growing into a huge ball before her, swollen, red as the fangs of a well-fed animal. Soon it would be dark, and that reminded her of the first thing she had forgotten to bring: a blanket. She stopped beneath a tree, dressed more warmly in additional clothing, and used one of the bags for a pillow. The roots in her back made her uncomfortable, and the stones, insects, twigs, and leaves made her itch and roll until she thought she would scream. It was dusk, and she was very tired. The first few stars came out, and she made a wish on one. She realized sadly that no one from the house of Michael and Constance had gone out in search of her, to bring her back. She settled down again and went to sleep. She slept soundly and her dreams, despite her surroundings and the drastic events of the day, were not in the least unusual.

Chapter Three

A Chance Meeting—Or Is It?

The sun rose, and the stars in the dark blue sky disappeared, one by one, as though they were absorbed, drawn together, losing their individual lights and adding together to make the great yellow fire that wakened Irene. She sat up, not being able at first to recall where she was. She hurt. Her arms and legs ached, and her back had stabbing pains that would not let her move in any way without paying for it with suffering. The stones and leaves clung to her black and gray clothing, and Irene spent a few minutes picking them clean. After another ten minutes, the pain had lessened and she was able to stand. She remembered now what she was doing. The sun reminded her. She had spent a long time the day before walking with the sun in her eyes as it set, westward. She was walking to California.

She was going to California to find a new cover for her Doric butter dish, to replace the one Alyse had deliberately broken.

Alyse had deliberately broken one of the few physical things that Irene loved. Why? wondered the old woman. Why would Alyse want to do that? Because of the trifling scene at the breakfast table? No, that couldn't be the reason. Irene didn't want to think that Alyse was that petty, that cruel. Alyse was too young.

And Irene was too old. She suddenly knew that the genuine horror of becoming old was not the approach of death. After all, death was approaching all through one's entire lifetime. Perhaps death's footfalls grew louder as one aged, but the threat was the same. The agony of getting old was that one had suffered so much in addition to the bodily deterioration. Others around the aging person began to expect less and demand less and appreciate less and love less and care less. The process of getting older carried an implicit burden of humiliation, as though the person had committed a social crime, an inexcusable outrage that was punishable only by banishment. Irene had been set apart. Michael and Constance had given her an entire wing of the house in which to be alone. They had explained that they wanted to protect her and guard her dignity, when in truth they had taken away the last bits of self-respect left to her. It would have been so much better if they had just let her live with the rest of the family. Getting old was not in itself the same thing as becoming a millstone around the necks of the young. It didn't have to be, but that was how the young interpreted the situation.

Irene started walking again, with the rising sun at her back. She tottered for a few minutes, and her legs hurt, and the two bundles she carried were very heavy. She sat down after a short time. She looked at herself. She was wearing a black dress with white dots on it. She had a purple shawl over that, which she had made more than twenty years before. She wore heavy black shoes and light gray stockings. Her white hair was pinned tightly to her head. Her arms were thin, too thin, she thought. She wondered when they had become that thin. They looked like broom handles, but not nearly as strong. Her arms were thin and yellowed, the skin was yellow, but the blue veins showed through clearly, and there were large brown spots on the skin. Her hands shook as she examined them. They looked fragile. They looked like they couldn't do any kind of work at all. She had no productive value left, and productive value was the only thing that had worth in the world. It was no wonder that Constance and Michael, yes, and Alyse, yes, and even Man and Woman treated her so. Irene had no productive value. There were weeds in the grass that had more value than she. The only possible benefit she could provide was as component chemical compounds returned to the soil after her death.

Death. It was a frequent theme in her thoughts.

She allowed herself a small breakfast, stood up, turned so that the sun was again at her back, and continued her walk toward California. She was very tired, and she hadn't walked more than half a mile since she started out that morning. She was very tired.

The world that she had left, the world of Michael's house, was a peaceful world, pastoral and simple. The eastern part of the continent was the same everywhere—cities had disappeared and the forest had reclaimed the land. Dwellings, farms, and ranches dotted the wooded landscape, widely scattered, rarely in touch with one another, independent and happy. And productive. Technology and industry, of the sort that had once been fashionable, had disappeared with the cities. Michael's home enjoyed the benefits of that technology, but after perfect machines, appliances, labor-saving devices had been developed, there was no longer any need for the technology. People tired of it, as they tired of any fancy that lost its charm. The Industrial Revolution, the Technocratic Revolution, both had become tiresome. The people themselves revolted, and life returned to the harmonious—Irene would say somnolent—level of the centuries before mechanical wonders replaced spiritual wonders. There were fewer people, far fewer. From the house of Michael and Constance, where Louisville had once stood, to the Atlantic Ocean, from Michael's house up to Maine and down to Florida, there were only two or three million people. These people were, for the most part, productive. Some, like Irene, were merely old. But that caused no one any great distress. The wonderful answer to the problem of aging was that the old would be dead soon. It was a crisis and a solution all in one.

But there was boredom. Irene saw it and heard it in Michael, in Constance, even in Alyse, who ought to be getting to the age when the world opened to her all its wonders. Irene was sure that Alyse had found not more than one tenth of the wonders that any young girl ought to have found. The world was better, surely. Better than what? Irene didn't care. The air was clean, and so was the water, and the forest was something like a religious temple to be in, to walk through. The birds and small animals impinged on Irene's consciousness. These were wonders that Alyse had yet to discover. These were things one appreciated only as one said good-bye to them.

How was Irene able to live in Michael's house? How did she presume to eat at his table, to sleep in the room in his house, to consume his resources, to smell his flowers, to hear his birds? As long as she could demonstrate that she was truly human, then she could live there guiltlessly. She was human because she had an occupation. She collected glass. It was a hobby, but in these days a hobby was a lifetime goal, a single defining program that gave purpose to each individual. Merely having and owning was a means of claiming productivity. Alyse had shattered Irene's productivity at the moment that the girl shattered the glass. Now Irene had a choice between death and restoring her identity, her programed purpose.

She would walk to California.

"You're tired, aren't you?" asked a man's voice from behind her.

Startled, Irene dropped her two bags and turned around. She gasped, but made no other sound.

"I'm sorry for coming up behind you like that," said the young man. He looked very embarrassed. "I don't know, sometimes, but I guess we're all entitled to a few mistakes. Startling older people. That's a great way to start off this trip."

"Excuse me?" asked Irene. She had never seen the young man before, and that meant that he was from very far away. She knew every person within hundreds of miles of Michael's house. She felt bad that he felt bad about startling her.

"Off on the wrong foot," he said, smiling. When he smiled, his teeth were dazzlingly white and clean. It gave his young face an expression of open honesty and cheerfulness. He was tall and slender, with his skin tanned dark, as though he were used to spending his days beneath the sun, tilling the soil, perhaps, or herding some form of living thing. He was well-muscled, dressed in a white robe. His hair was blond and cut short, in a style unlike that of Michael and all the other young men Irene had known in the last few decades. His eyes were the most fascinating thing about him. They were brown eyes, soft brown, and they held Irene's attention, even while she tried to get an idea of his personality from his other physical attributes. She noticed his strong hands, and then her eyes returned to his. She noticed the well-developed muscles of his legs, and her eyes sought his. The handsome face—and again her eyes looked into his. He smiled again. "But," he said, "that's over with. Nothing to do about it now, is there? Just say 'I'm sorry for startling you, ma'am,' and we can begin again. Is that all right? Will you forgive me, Miss Irene?"

"Forgive you?" asked Irene.

The young man's smile went away. "If I am to guide you, ma'am, you'll have to forgive me. It's part of the way it works. You have to forgive me."

Irene stared at him for a moment. She wondered why he was wearing a robe. It looked thin, almost transparent, and she guessed that he would be very cold in it. It was only April, and in the mornings and the late evenings it could still frost. Her thoughts were beginning to wander.

"Miss Irene," said the young man firmly, "do you forgive me for startling you on the road?"

"Yes, yes, of course," she said. "It was nothing."

"Well, it was something. Small, but something. But now it's all gone, all taken care of, and we can begin again. Good morning, Miss Irene, good morning."

She smiled. He reached to take her bags. "Good morning," she said. "How do you know my name?"

The young man nodded. His smile was mysterious now, not the open and honest smile he had shown earlier. "My name is Glorian," he said. "I am called Glorian of the Knowledge. In Latin that would be Glorianus Scientiae, but I don't use that except on formal occasions."

"Glorian," said Irene. She tried to recall what that name meant to her. She knew it meant something, but her memory was not as reliable as it had been in her youth. "Glorian," she said, "haven't I read about you before?"

He smiled shyly.

"I thought I knew that name," said Irene. "I could have sworn it. Glorian of the Knowledge. There can't be too many people running around with a name like that. Yes, now I remember. What brings you to this little grassy path, which is leading me westward to my fate?"

"You do, of course."

"Of course." Irene was a bit worried. She had thought that she would set out for California, and whether or not she made it she would die in the attempt, and it would be a good death and a proper finish to her life. Now, though, with the addition of Glorian, things took on a weight and a significance that she really didn't need or want.

"I'm to lead you through your trials," he said, "across the vast distance, and present you before your judges, where your personal worth, moral integrity, and so forth will be weighed and your reward or punishment will be decided."

"Never mind that," said Irene. "I don't want to hear anything about it. I'm going to California to find the home of Mrs. Elizabeth Dawson Douglas in Springfield, and I'm going to look through her marvelous collection of twentieth-century Depression glass, now very old and dusty, and I'm going to replace the top to my Doric butter dish, now smashed and broken, and then I'm going home. My personal worth and my rewards and punishments are entirely beyond the scope of my little adventure."

"No, they're not," said Glorian. He smiled his boyish smile again. "You see, you're on something important. You've begun a true quest, and you have to follow it through, no matter what happens. I'm your Virgil, as it were, and we have a prescribed set of circumstances. You'll have dangers and threats and temptations, just as every hero does, and you'll have treasures beyond your greatest fantasies waiting for you at the end of the journey. This isn't my first heroic saga, you know. I've known and guided some of the all-time greats. The fact that I'm here at all should make you proud. It says something about your inner worth."

Irene frowned. "I'd appreciate it if you'd go away. I'm not thinking at all about having an adventure or a saga or anything like that. I'm out for a pleasant walk to California. I'm sure that there must be other worthy heroes and heroines out there who could use your help."

Glorian closed his eyes and rubbed his forehead. He opened his beautiful brown eyes and gazed at Irene for several seconds in silence. "You must understand," he said. "It's gone beyond choosing. You don't really have any say in the matter now. You couldn't turn around and go home, not for any reason. It would be physically impossible. Just try. I dare you. I double-dog dare you."

Irene was getting a little annoyed. Glorian was treating her like a child, which is one of the ways that younger people treat older people—like children. It was one of the things that she hated most about living in the house of Michael and Constance. "All right," she said, "I will. Which way is home?"

"That way," said Glorian, pointing one long beautiful arm, graceful wrist, well-shaped hand, and classic forefinger.

"Good morning, Glorian," said Irene. "It's been a pleasure and an honor to meet you. Really. If you will give me back my two parcels, I'll be on my way. They probably miss me at the house. They're probably worried to death."

"They don't give a hoot in a holler," he said.

Irene didn't answer. She took her two bags and tried to set off in the direction Glorian indicated. She couldn't. She just couldn't move her body at all. "I see what you mean," she said.

"An adventure," said Glorian. "A thrilling tale of excitement. Physical dangers. Mental dangers. Spiritual dangers. Grand perils and grander prizes. You can't imagine."

"Yes, I can," said Irene sadly. "I just don't want to."

"Look at it this way," said Glorian, taking her two bags again. "You don't even know where California is, do you?"

"No."

"I do. You don't know how far it is, do you?"

"No," she said.

"It's two thousand, two hundred miles, just about."

"How far is that?"

Glorian thought for a moment. "You know the gravel driveway from Michael's house to the road? That's about a quarter of a mile. If you walked it, turned around and walked back, turned around again and walked to the road, then turned around and went back to the house, that would be a mile."

"Lord," said Irene. "I'd be worn out."

Glorian smiled kindly. "Just think how tired you'd be if you made the same expedition from house to road eight thousand, eight hundred times. That's the equivalent of your journey to California."

Irene's face paled. "Eight thousand, you say?"

"Nearly nine thousand."

Irene hesitated. "That's a long way," she said after a moment.

"If you did it once a day," said Glorian, "the mile, I mean, it would take you six years to get to California."

"Six years!" Irene shook her head. She couldn't go home, and the idea of taking six years to get to California stunned her.

"Well, we can shorten it. At two miles per day, that's three years. At four miles per day, it would take only a year and a half. That's not so bad, is it? It's what? April? A year from next Halloween and you'll be in California. And some days we can go more than four miles. It's not so bad. We can average a lot more than four miles a day, especially with me helping you along, cooking for you, guiding you through the dangers and hazards and monsters and wild, desperate men who haunt the roads, and the traps, and the pitfalls set to snare the immoral and the—"

"I can't go home," said Irene. "You've already demonstrated that. But rather than go through this tedious appraisal of what I have to look forward to, I think I'd rather just get on with it. Keep the bags if you want them. I'll just go on ahead."

"I have to accompany you, Miss Irene," said Glorian.

"I don't think so," said Irene. "I can take care of myself."

"I don't think so," said Glorian. "You can't even carry these things."

"Then drop them. Or give them away."

"And you don't know the direction."

"That way," said Irene. "I can't go in the wrong direction. Something won't let me."

"And that something won't let you go in the right direction without me. Please. I don't like this any more than you. I have other ways of spending time. But let's try to make the best of it. We'll grow fond of each other as the months pass. And as I've hinted, there are definitely going to be horrible things ahead, and I know them all. I've been there and back. I can let you in on the secrets that will get you by most of the terrifying things waiting to snatch you."

"*Most* of them?" asked Irene.

"They change them from time to time," said Glorian. He looked down at his feet, embarrassed.

"Fine," said Irene. "You will take me to California?"

Glorian looked up, a great smile of satisfaction and relief on his face. "Would you mind signing this?" he asked.

"What is it?"

"A form," he said. "A standard form. A release, and a kind of contract, and you say that you've agreed to the terms, and a no-fault anti-indemnity thing, and you've said that you will accept me as your initiator, and so on."

"Where did it come from?" asked Irene. "You don't have any pockets in that robe, do you?"

"Here," said Glorian, handing her the form and pen. She took them, glanced briefly at the contract, and signed it. Glorian signed it, and put the paper and pen away. Irene watched him closely, trying to see where he put them, but she couldn't discover his secret. "So," he said, taking a deep breath, "the preliminaries are over, and we may begin."

"How do we do that?" asked Irene. She didn't feel up to facing a peril so early in the day.

"This way," said Glorian. He bowed and pointed down the grassy lane, and Irene walked by him. He followed closely, carrying her two bags.

"California," said Irene. "I wonder what it will be like."

"I could tell you," said Glorian, "but it would spoil the surprise." They walked on in silence for some time. Irene had many things to think about. Glorian walked about a step and a half behind her. He whistled, hummed, or sang to himself the whole time. Irene wondered if she could stand that for a year and a half. Or less, if they averaged more than four miles per day.

"The whole idea of this thing is crazy, you know," Irene said some time later. "I never should have done it. I should have stayed home and just dried up and let the wind blow me away. I should have sneaked back into the house before anyone knew what I was doing, or else they would all have laughed at me. This is crazy."

Glorian stopped humming. He had been humming an ancient tune called, "Never Should Have Told You," a tune he loved especially. "It's not crazy to follow your dream," he said. "It's not crazy to yearn to be free. It's never crazy to go out and make the big play, the real, true, absolute quest for the grand design. It's not crazy at all."

"It is if you're eighty-two years old," said Irene.

"I'm quite a bit older than that myself, Miss Irene."

"Oh? How old are you, then?"

"I'm not at liberty to say," said Glorian pleasantly. "That's part of my identity, you know. But written records of my little exploits appeared hundreds and hundreds of years ago, back when the world, this part of the world, was very, very different. So eighty-two isn't so advanced an age for an adventurer."

Irene stopped and faced him. "You're a mythological creature," she said. "You're a symbol and a legend. You're a piece of folklore.

You're a spirit. You're Puck and Robin Goodfellow. That's why you're so old. I'm a woman. I'm an eighty-two-year-old woman who is staggering along at a very slow pace in search of something completely silly."

Glorian didn't know quite how to take her remarks. He didn't know whether he should be flattered or angry. "Legend, eh?" he said. "You bet your life I'm a legend, and with good reason. A symbol, maybe not. Folklore, that depends on popular opinion. You have to be accepted generally to be a piece of folklore. I wouldn't have enough votes. And as for mythological, well, just poke me. Go on. Go ahead, poke me."

Irene shook her head. She turned around and walked on down the barely visible path.

"What's wrong?" asked Glorian. "Have I made you upset?"

"No," she said. "I'm telling you that you're not there, while I'm making you carry the two bags. I'm very sorry, Glorian."

He laughed. "Everything is fine," he said. "The day is nice and warm, we have a pleasant country to hike through, we have each other for company and conversation, we have a goal, we have a mission, and neither of us has left anything of importance behind."

Irene opened her mouth to disagree, then realized that in fact she didn't disagree. "What was that tune you were humming before?" she asked.

"This one?" said Glorian, humming a few bars of "String of Pearls."

"No," said Irene.

"I don't remember, then. And no one ever again will laugh at you for doing what your spirit tells you to do. I will see to that. From now on your inner promptings will be your guide. You are pure, Miss Irene, you are acceptable to the infrastructure complex that governs the world and the universe, and I have been sent to ease your passage from mere life to a more glorious existence."

"All I want is a piece of green glass," said Irene. "I really have little use for an infrastructure, unless they're shelves. I've always been short of shelf space. Then I could bring more glass home with me. It would be wonderful if I could get the other two pieces of the Shirley Temple set."

"Ah!" cried Glorian, in such a tone that Irene stopped and turned to look at him. "You know Shirley Temple?"

Irene shook her head. "No," she said, "not personally."

"But you know of her? She belongs to the ages, to the era of greatness, when this country and nation was at its highest degree of power and glory. Shirley Temple! Almost a goddess, her name is magical enough to keep marauding predators away from our camp all night. And you have had contact, no matter how rarefied, with another piece of folklore."

"Do you have meetings, or conventions, or anything?" asked Irene. She imagined all the various demigods and partial deities and symbolic creatures standing around in groups talking, getting drinks, listening to speeches, applauding, eating dinner together, going back to their hotel rooms, talking about others who were not there, getting drunk and talking loudly, bothering the poor humans on Earth. That might explain a lot, thought Irene. Earthquakes possibly, thunderstorms, things like that.

"No," said Glorian, "but we ought to. Just to keep up with what is going on around the universe. I'm amazed sometimes at how much I've missed, particularly when I'm on call, like now. When this is all finished in a year or so, I'll go back and there will be new faces all around, and old friends who will be gone... ." His voice trailed off.

Irene was sorry that she had started a sad train of thought "How do you get your assignments?" she asked. "From whom?"

"I don't really know," said Glorian. "I'm not all that high in the hierarchy, you know. Even though I've been at it for a long time, there seems to be hundreds, thousands of others with more seniority. I get orders in a plain white legal-sized envelope, unsigned. I just do what I'm told. Yesterday the envelope had a page describing you and where you're going and why, and what I'm supposed to do about it and—"

"Can I see it?"

Glorian's eyes widened. "Heaven's sakes, no!" he said, astonished. "That would be disastrous. The letter went up in smoke and flames after I read it. Some kind of sloppy universe we'd be running if plain people started getting the inside information."

Irene smiled serenely. She was very happy. She liked Glorian, and she knew that she presented a problem to him. He didn't know how to handle her. His previous experiences must have been simple, ordinary bits of heroic chronicle. Helping a little old lady across the street—across the continent—would be something new to him. That made her feel very good. Michael and Constance were bored with her, Alyse was full of hostility. Glorian, though, would not exhaust her years of experience in the eighteen months they would spend together. Irene had a long lifetime's worth of living, of a kind that Glorian had never before encountered. Irene was as much a riddle to him as he was to her. That was wonderful.

"There are things I'd like explained," she said. "If we're really going to do this thing, then I think I have a right to know a little more about the situation. What do you mean by 'country,' 'world,' and 'universe'? These are words that haven't any definite meanings, at least as far as my poor human understanding is concerned. Sometimes I feel angry, and sometimes helpless. At home, Michael's, I was pitied. I hated that. I don't want revenge, or even justice. I don't know really what I want. And you have orders to guide me, and I don't even know what I'm doing or why. Do you know?"

"I am Glorian of the Knowledge," he said, just a trifle smugly. "I could hardly be of the Knowledge if I didn't know."

"Could you tell me, then?"

He sighed. "Then you would be Miss Irene of the Knowledge, and there's no room in the pantheon for that."

"I don't want all the Knowledge," she said. "Just what concerns me personally."

"The Knowledge is inseparable," said Glorian.

"Come on, let's get going," said Irene. "That remark doesn't mean a doggone thing." She was more than a little annoyed.

"I'm sorry," said Glorian. He started to hum again.

"I only know that I have to do something or die," murmured Irene. "Now he tells me that it's possible that I have to do something *and* die. I guess I suspected that before. It's all the same to me."

They walked on through the forest. Birds flew by overhead, chirping, making flitting shadows on the sun-splashed ground. Insects buzzed in the trees. Glorian pointed out the various sounds, and described the kinds of creatures that made them. He caught a skink for her, and showed it to Irene.

"It's beautiful," she said, looking at the coppery lizard in Glorian's hand. "I've seen them before, but I didn't know what they were called."

Glorian set it down in the grass and watched it hurry away. "I love animals," he said thoughtfully.

"Are they called skinks because when they run they slink and skitter?" she asked.

"That's terrible," said Glorian, looking up at her. "They're called skinks from the Latin *scincus*, from the verb *scindere*, to cut or split. The ancients all thought that lizards left their tails in your hand if you grabbed them. Rome must have been infested with thousands of abbreviated lizards."

"The Knowledge," said Irene.

"I'm sorry," said Glorian, standing up and wiping his hands on his white robe. "I'm sorry if my comprehension of these things makes you uncomfortable. That's just the way it is."

"No, no," said Irene, laughing. "I love it! The Knowledge! It makes me glad just to know that there is a Knowledge." Glorian smiled at her. They continued their walk. It was well past noon, and he wanted to reach a certain part of the forest before late afternoon. They would make camp there, and there was a small stream nearby. Irene walked on, still overcome by the excitement and the beauty and the hints of profound truths to be learned. Behind her, Glorian whistled a tune. Irene couldn't grasp the melody. Glorian, for all his Knowledge, was a poor whistler.

They reached the clearing two hours later. The sun was blazing orange as it dropped lower in the sky, like a distant fire beyond the broad leaves of the trees. Glorian suggested that Irene rest at the foot of a large oak while he prepared their dinner. "Let me do something," she said.

"It's all right," he said. "I can put together a meal by myself much quicker without your help."

Irene felt suddenly cold. "Your Knowledge, again?" she asked bitterly. "I'm too old. I'll get in your way. I'm just an old woman, and I should sit here and be fed, like a senile crazy old lady in the bin."

Glorian looked up. "No," he said, "you have it all wrong."

"I'm glad," she said. She didn't sound as though she meant it.

"Really," he said. "Look." He held up two plates. There were mounds of pasta shells mixed with a tomato and meat sauce, covered with melted mozzarella cheese.

Irene was startled. She said nothing. She didn't know where Glorian had found the plates, the pasta, the sauce, or the cheese. There hadn't been a fire to cook the things, and there hadn't been any time. For a moment, Irene was afraid of Glorian.

"I'm sorry, but I don't have any silverware," he said, bringing a plate over to her. She took it. The food smelled incredibly good. She hadn't eaten anything like it in years. She just held the plate and looked at the food. Glorian opened one of her bags and got out a spoon for her to use. She hardly paid attention. She ate quickly, realizing suddenly that she was very hungry. She didn't even watch to see how Glorian ate his food. When she was finished eating, he was finished, too. He took the two plates and walked toward the stream, about thirty yards away on the other side of the clearing. "Look," he said, pointing upward, "a cardinal."

Irene looked up and saw a flash of red in the leaves above. When she looked down again, Glorian was gone. She was sleepy now, after the meal. She thought about how far she had walked that day. She tried to clear a place to lie down, scrabbling the stones and sticks away. Then she just put her head down on the matted leaves and grass. She was asleep almost immediately. She slept soundly, awakening only once during the night to pull the blanket up closer to her chin. In her sleep, she didn't wonder where the blanket had come from.

Chapter Four

Never Too Old

"Good morning, Miss Irene! Good morning, good morning!"

Irene awoke. Her eyes were bleary, and when she sat up there was a sharp pain in her back that made her cry out. Her arms, legs, and joints ached so much that she knew she'd never be able to stand upright again.

"Are you in pain, Miss Irene?" asked Glorian. She nodded, wincing. "It is my fault, then. I've forgotten your advanced age. Unforgivable. A horrible mistake. I have brought you pain instead of guidance. I have led you into a danger where there was no danger. The times will be difficult enough without my stupidity. Forgive me, Miss Irene, please forgive me."

"Yes, Glorian," she said in a soft voice. She hurt very much.

"I don't know if I'm supposed to get that in writing," he said, pacing the small clearing. "Less than a full day out, and already I'm improvising. At least I can take away the pain."

"Would you do that, please, Glorian?" she asked.

"Of course," he said. He came next to her, put one hand on her shoulder, and smiled.

"Oh!" cried Irene. "It's wonderful! I haven't felt this way in many, many years! I feel young! I feel whole!"

"It won't last," said Glorian sadly. "The pain is gone and won't come back. But your normal disabilities will return in about half an hour."

"Then let's do something in the meantime!"

Glorian looked at her thoughtfully. "What would you like to do?"

"I don't know," she said.

"I don't, either." He was glad that she hadn't suggested physical intimacy. "We could get your first trial out of the way. You have to have a kind of initiation, which you will most probably fail. It would all be easier on you now."

Irene frowned. "I told you yesterday that I refuse to go on an adventure. I'm just casually walking through the woods to California. I didn't ask for your company, and I don't feel obliged to take part in your dramatic scenes."

Glorian sat down in the dewy grass beside her. "Let me take that," he said, folding up the navy blanket and putting it—

"Where did you put that?" cried Irene.

"Away," said Glorian.

"Where? Stand up." Glorian stood up, and the blanket was nowhere to be seen. It wasn't concealed in his loose white robe, either.

"Forget that," he said. "Look at it this way. Your home, the house of Michael and Constance, I mean, was a kind of womb. Some people would see it that way. Doctors would see it that way. You were protected in the house, and fed, and all your needs and wants were satisfied, and you didn't have to do anything at all."

"I was waiting to die," she said in a somber voice.

"Yes, indeed," said Glorian. "That proves my point, in a way. In this circumstance, your death would have been removal from the womb. Your death would have been your birth. Traumatic, either way. But your birth has come about in another mode entirely. By leaving the house on your own, you have been born into the world. Do you follow that?"

Irene nodded. "You've been doing some studying since your last adventures, haven't you?"

Glorian nodded shyly. "Now, my part," he said, "is to persuade you that the peace of the womb has not been lost eternally, that it can be returned to you under the proper conditions. Almost all myths and legends and psychological problems stem from feeling of having lost something that is irreplaceable. The womb. The safety and security of the womb. Once you're born, wacko!, it's gone, and you spend the rest of your life trying to get it back. The Garden of Eden was the womb. See?"

"Of course, of course," said Irene.

"And now you have to go through this preset series of trials. The prize is the Garden of Eden. Heaven. The womb. Happiness. Whatever you feel like."

"I feel like having breakfast."

"Here," said Glorian, giving her a large bowl of cereal with milk and sugar and strawberries. "The spoon is in one of your bags."

"What kind of adventure do I have today?" she asked.

"A small one. A tiny one, in fact, compared with the ones coming up later. By the way, that's about all the food I can provide today. I have a daily allotment, you see. I'm not all-powerful, you know."

Irene gave him a warm smile. "I know," she said, "and I'm grateful. Thank you so much for the blanket last night."

"It's all right," he said. "I wish I could have given you a pillow."

"You're very nice, Glorian."

He looked down at the ground and pushed some leaves around with a sandal-clad foot. "As to the adventure, let me see if I can devise something fitting and not terribly taxing. You will have to learn that power is within you yourself, that I am nothing but the projection of your own strength. You don't believe that now, but by the time we get to California, you will, I'm sure. Otherwise the whole thing is a failure and a waste of time, and you will just plain die, and I'll have to face a board of inquiry, and we might as well just stop right here and now."

"Why don't we just stop right here and now?" asked Irene.

"Because I have faith in you," said Glorian.

Irene finished eating her breakfast. Glorian took the bowl and put it where he had put the blanket. Irene shook her head. "You have faith in me," she said. "Wouldn't it be better if I had faith in you? You tell me that I'm capable of doing these things, but when I look at myself, all that I see is a shriveled old woman. Look, look at my arms." She held her arms out in front of her. They shook with an uncontrollable palsy. "How thin I am, how weak I am closer to death than life," she said.

"Trust me," said Glorian.

"I do trust you," she said, "but I don't trust myself. I'm not on a quest, Glorian, no matter what you say. You're trying to force yourself into my life. You're trying to take my old age and use it for whatever purposes you have. I won't be used like that, Glorian."

There was a tense silence in the forest. "If you put it like that," said Glorian after a moment, "I have to agree. If that were true, I'd pack up and leave, and you could spend five or six days dying in the forest, and no one would ever hear from you again. But it isn't true. You have a destiny, Miss Irene. You are meant for more than dropping dead among the sheltering monarchs of this great woodland. You are intended for more than decomposing into rich topsoil."

Irene sighed. "Who decided that destiny for me, Glorian? You? Who decided that I was meant for more? Who decided what I was intended for? It wasn't me, that's for sure. And I don't see why I have to be bound by someone else's decisions. It's my life."

"It's not," said Glorian. "Ever since you left the house, it's been something else. You left the womb. You're alive now, Miss Irene, and you have to accept the consequences."

Irene stared at him and took a long, deep breath. "Then let's get going. What's first?"

"As I said, you have a kind of initiation. You get your feet wet, kind of. A sort of baptism of fire, nothing very difficult, just an indication of the way things will be going from now on. I'll be with you every step of the way, and if you will just follow my advice, we'll get you to California just as easy as pie."

Irene was still upset and very doubtful. "Let me see your hands, Glorian," she said. He held his hands out, puzzled. She examined his hands and his fingernails. "Look," she said, pointing at white marks on the fingernails.

"Moons," he said. "They look like crescent moons."

"Clouds," she said, "and they tell the future."

"No," said Glorian, "you can't tell the future. I can tell the future, but you can't."

"Here, on your left hand, your ring finger. There's a white mark nearly at the edge. When it reaches the quick, it means that you will make someone else happy. Every finger has a meaning, you see, and the prediction comes true when the cloud reaches the edge."

"That's nonsense," said Glorian. "That can't be true, or they would have taught us about that."

"Forget it, then, dear. I'm just an old crazy lady, so don't pay any attention to what I have to say." She began walking away from him, toward the stream. She had decided to follow the water downstream, where it would eventually empty into a larger river. That way she wouldn't get lost, and wouldn't end up spending the last days of her life circling the same trees in the vast and unbroken forest.

Glorian stood behind, still holding his hands out in front of him. He shrugged and hurried to catch up with her. "Miss Irene!" he called. "Stop for a minute. Let me show you this."

Irene stopped and turned around. She had a feeling that if her life was going to stay under her control, she would have to make Glorian realize for once and for all that she knew what she wanted, and that she would not be forced away from her original plan.

Glorian stopped in front of her. He held out something for her. She took it and saw that it was a small pamphlet. The cover was a light gray color. The words on it were printed in blue.

Heroic Behavior

SOME DO'S AND DONTS

At the bottom of the cover, in black ink, were the words Powers That Be Printing Office. Publication No. 6014-B.

"*Heroic Behavior?*" asked Irene.

"*Heroic Behavior,*" said Glorian. "There is a right way to go about this, and a wrong way. You're not the first person who has shouted defiance at the gods, you know. You're not the first person who has tried to wrest free the great gift of truth that the gods themselves keep as their own. You're not the first person who has taken up the challenge of Nature, of the spiritual world beyond life and death. Others have gone before you. Some have succeeded, and their names are familiar to schoolchildren around the world, throughout the centuries. Such folk as Prometheus, Odysseus, Porcellus Tarvin, Johnny Appleseed, and Robert Wayne Hanson have given their all and won everlasting honor. Others have tried and failed, but the trying alone is enough to mark them as special. No, Irene, you are not alone. You have the trail marked by those who have gone ahead of you. You have me, Glorian of the Knowledge, to ease your way past the more disconcerting dangers. And you have this pamphlet, which I can assure you was not available to Prometheus and some of the others."

"Am I responsible for all this material?" asked Irene, as she leafed through the booklet.

"Yes," said Glorian. "Every bit of it. You will be tested, again and again."

"I want to go home."

"You can't go home."

"I don't want to read this," she said, throwing it on the ground.

"Miss Irene!" cried Glorian. He bent over and picked up the pamphlet. "If you show no respect for the Powers That Be, they will show no respect for you."

"That's petty of them," she said. "None of this is my choosing in the first place."

"All of it is your choosing. Let's just look at the first page, and maybe we'll get an idea of how simple it will be. Look. The first section is called 'What Is a Hero?'"

Irene stood a little apart from Glorian. She was very unhappy. She felt that after eighty-two years of life, she should be able to decide for herself how to end that life. She did not even want to belong to the ranks of near gods like Odysseus and Johnny Appleseed. Not Irene. She had had a more peaceful end in mind. But she listened as Glorian read to her.

"'What is a hero?'" he read. "'Well, in answer to this simple question, there is a multitude of answers. Everything depends primarily upon circumstance. What would be heroic behavior in one situation could very possibly be unheroic, even cowardly behavior in another situation. How is one to tell the difference? How is one to decide if the situation calls for heroic action, or some other response? That is what this little treatise is designed to answer. In the following pages, we will try to shed a little light on these problems. We will try to help along the aspiring hero (or heroine, of course! Let there be no doubt that there have been a goodly number of female personalities who have sought and found eternal glory, in one way or another). We will try to sort out the truth from the overwhelming bushels of chaff that cloud the individual's eyes whenever the subjective matter of heroism and valor is considered. These things and more are the subject of this booklet, but supplemental publications, obtainable from the Powers That Be Printing Office for a nominal fee to cover postage and handling, will go into this area in greater detail and in considerable depth.'"

"Glorian?" asked Irene.

"Yes, Miss Irene?"

"Please stop reading that."

Glorian looked up. "It's very urgent that you know this subject matter. You are going to be presented with challenge after challenge, and you can't hope to compete with evil unless you're well informed."

"I don't want to compete with evil. I'm eighty-two years old, and the whites of my eyes have turned yellow."

"You have no choice."

"You're well informed, aren't you, Glorian?" she asked.

"Certainly."

"Then before every challenge, you tell me what I ought to do."

Glorian paused. He thought this over. "That just wouldn't carry any weight with a regular hero," he said. "But, as you say, you're a special case. You're of advanced years, and surely entitled to a little outside advice. All right, then, if you'll trust my judgment."

"Implicitly," she said, "if we can just throw that book away."

"I'll keep it for reference," said Glorian. Together they began the day's march toward California.

After a couple of hours, during which they said little to each other beside pointing out rocks, trees, shrubs, flowers, birds, insects, cloud formations, sounds, and fungi of interest, Glorian, who had been walking at his customary step and a half behind Irene, suggested that they stop for lunch.

"You can't supply anything more for lunch," said Irene, recalling what he had told her at breakfast. "And I have only a little food in that one bag."

"It's enough for a good lunch," said Glorian.

Irene turned around to say something, but before the words were spoken she gasped. Glorian had changed. He was no longer a tall, darkly tanned, well-muscled blond youth with strong white teeth.

He was a kid.

He was a young boy, about eight years old. He had brown hair and brown eyes, and he had braces on his teeth. He was a good deal shorter than Irene, who was not particularly tall herself. He was dressed in a blue uniform with a yellow neckerchief, and a blue cap. Sewn on the uniform's shirt were various strips and badges and devices. Irene could see that Glorian—it must be Glorian, she thought—belonged to Cub Scout Pack Fourteen, Den One, from Hamilton Square, New Jersey. Glorian had earned his Bobcat badge and his Wolf badge, and he had one gold arrow and one silver arrow. He looked very proud and handsome in his uniform, but he was young. He seemed too young to be leading someone of Irene's age across the trackless jungle of North America.

"Glorian?" she asked. Her voice was a little hoarse. She didn't react to surprises such as this as readily as she used to.

"Yes, Miss Irene, it's still me." He saluted her with the Cub Scout salute, which was touching his cap's bill with the forefinger and middle finger of his right hand.

"You want to make lunch now?"

"Yes, Miss Irene," he said. He knelt and opened the bag.

Irene thought that Glorian looked—well, she searched her memory for a few moments, trying to decide just *how* he looked. He looked cute, or sweet, or something like that, but she knew he would be hurt if she told him so. She watched him preparing their meager store of food. "What's that you're wearing, dear?" she asked.

He looked over his shoulder and smiled. "It's a Cub Scout uniform," he said. "It belongs to the same time period as the glass you collect. I have the Wolf Badge, so I'm acquainted somewhat with the woods, and what it takes to survive in them. I thought that would be the best thing. Generally on these journeys my companions are every bit as woodswise as I am, if not more so. But this time around, I guess I'll have to take things in hand for your comfort and your traveling pleasure."

"I appreciate it, Glorian, but it makes me nervous when you change into other things."

Glorian stood up. He was still very short. He was just a boy. "Don't worry about that, Miss Irene," he said. "I won't do much changing. Just whenever the climate of our relationship dictates. For now, I'm just going to be a young man helping you along until suppertime tonight."

"You're cute, Glorian, you really are," said Irene, not caring at all if it bothered him. She smiled. He frowned.

"This Wolf badge and the arrow points mean that I've completed an arduous process of initiation of my own," he said. "You have an arduous initiation, and if I were you, I'd be boning up on it. The booklet wasn't printed up just to give people jobs, you know."

Irene sat down, sighing. "Just what do I have to do to get to California?" she asked.

Glorian, little Glorian, took off his Cub Scout cap and scratched his head. "It's not just getting to California," he said. "You don't understand. If it was just getting to California, we'd just walk. But the threshold is guarded by spirits of the somatosphere, and beyond that the way is threatened by physical apparitions of the psychosphere. Or the other way around. I don't remember which, and it doesn't make any difference."

"What threshold?"

Glorian sat beside her and offered her an orange. She didn't question where it came from. She took it gratefully and peeled it while he spoke. "You see," he said, "you're gradually moving from the world and life you used to know into something different. Not just space and distance, but in the quality of the mystical emanations. And the quantity. There are more mystical emanations around us right now than you've probably ever noticed in your whole lifetime."

"I've never noticed them and I don't notice them now," she said. She spit out a seed.

"They're here, all right," said Glorian. "Don't make any mistake about that. And they're all watching. If you cross the threshold, you'll be safe from them but in danger from others. If you turn back or away from the threshold, they've got you."

"Got me how?"

Glorian's eight-year-old face paled. He couldn't answer.

"Where is the threshold?" asked Irene.

"Do you really want to know?"

"I want to get it over with," she said.

"Good! Great! I was hoping you'd say that!" He stood up and helped Irene to her feet. "The threshold is just over there," he said, indicating a white birch tree. "Walk past it maybe two, three feet."

"That's all?"

"Yes, but be careful. The meal will be ready when you get back."

Irene shrugged. She drew her shawl around her a little closer and walked to the birch. She turned and saw little Glorian arranging twigs, evidently to start a small fire. Irene turned again, put one hand on the birch, took a step—

—into the 125th Street Station of the IND subway line in New York City.

"Hah!" she cried. The bright lights, the hard surfaces, the roar and clamor of the place, the immense crowds, the words in huge letters threatening her from signs everywhere, the almost irresistible flow of people moving in currents in even' direction, the foul smells, even the taste of the air made her ill. She knew real terror, for the first time in her life, in her long life.

Irene stooped down—her joints, which ached earlier in the day, now absolutely refused to function without a fight, and her eyesight had been halved, and her hearing was of a kind of blurry nature, and her back was stiff, and everything about her body creaked whenever it had the opportunity—and picked up the handles of the two shopping bags. She didn't know why. She just did, as though they were part of her, of her identity. Something in her mind told her that she was correct, that the shopping bags were indeed part of her identity, a large part, more of her identity than her clothing, her appearance, her voice, or the way in which she had spent the eight decades of her life on Earth.

Irene muttered to herself. She was shocked inside; she found that she was able to watch herself from within, keep an internal commentary of her sensory impressions and evaluations and thoughts. She was disgusted by the new form she had been thrust into. She muttered just softly enough so that no one nearby could understand, just loudly enough so that everyone nearby could tell that she was a crazy old lady. Her mouth was almost toothless and the taste there was so bad that if she had been given the option, Irene would have done without the mouth altogether. The tongue felt like a smooth and dead piece of leather. Her eyes squinted and her nose had sniffles. She muttered, carrying the two ancient shopping bags up and down the station platform, looking for a place to sit down. It was apparently a busy time of day, and all the benches were occupied. She stood next to one, muttering, and waited for a subway train to come into the station. People from the bench dashed for the open doors, and people from the open doors dashed for the bench. Irene swung her shopping bags in a threatening arc and sat down on the end of the bench. There was a gap beside her; no one wanted to sit there because of her bags and her muttering. She had a large part of the bench all to herself. She put the shopping bags, which were reinforced with twine and string and clothesline, between her feet. She started to look through them. There was only trash.

Irene wondered why Glorian had chosen this as her initiation into the ancient mysteries he represented. She thought that he might not have been responsible for the actual test, that something higher up was to blame. She made a mental note to have words with that being at first opportunity. Irene felt disgraced and, even worse, she felt soiled in her soul. This place was not fit for good people. The noise and the constant motion and total strangeness tortured her.

Irene watched herself tugging at her clothing, her tattered and unbearably filthy clothing, pulling up her hose, scratching at the sleeves of the worn dress, muttering all the while. Irene watched from inside as the outside Irene, the shopping-bag lady, got up and provoked an argument with a waste receptacle. There had been a copy of the *New York Post* in the waste receptacle, which the outside Irene had salvaged for her shopping bags, but the newspaper wasn't complete. The back pages, the sports section, was missing. She blamed the waste receptacle for that, and she did so at great length and with an energy and a strange satisfaction that the inner Irene had never known.

"Let me out of here!" cried Irene from inside.

"Listen, you pervert, creep," said Irene from the outside, talking to a space empty of everything, "who do you think you are? Who do you think you're talking to?"

"Please, Glorian!"

"You think I'm some kind of idiot, right? Don't you? And you think you can pull one off on the old lady, right? Forget it, creep. I been around. I seen."

Irene on the inside was beginning to calm down, as the initial horror lessened just a little. There was a cultural shock, and an identity shock, and a temporal shock, and the shock of sudden displacement and sudden separation and sudden, intense loneliness—

Loneliness. That was the key. Irene, on the inside, felt it.

Irene on the outside: "Just because I'm standing here, right, you think that gives you the right, just because I'm standing here. Let me tell you, creep, I been standing here. I know. I know. I been around, creep. I seen."

The inner Irene: "Glorian?"

"Yes?" It was Glorian's voice, coming from somewhere, sometime, in Irene's mind.

"Glorian, is this real? Are there *places* like this? Are there *people* like this?"

"Yes," said Glorian. "Remember your Bible."

The trapped Irene knew what he meant. Hell, she thought. Loneliness. Being cut off from everyone and everything. Being separate all through eternity. Hell. This old Irene, this damaged body and meager mind and corrupted senses and filthy life and her two shopping bags of refuse, and the eternal inability to *not* be lonely.

Loneliness. Intense isolation unlike anything she could imagine.

Irene let her breath out in a gasp. She was back in the clean forest, back in her own clean body, back with Glorian who, unfortunately, was still an eight-year-old boy in a Cub Scout uniform. She needed comforting, and the boy wouldn't understand.

Irene forgot that beneath the suit of blue was the heart of Glorian, and he understood. He held her while she cried. She cried for many minutes.

"All right, now?" he asked later.

"Glorian," said Irene, "what about that woman? The old woman?"

"She's still there," said Glorian. "In hell. With many, many others."

"Can't we do anything for them?"

There was silence in the forest. Night had fallen, and inserts buzzed and chirred around them. Glorian made an elaborate and nourishing dinner for them. He led her to the table he had prepared from logs. Irene clung to the boy's arm. "Can't we do anything for them?" she asked again.

The boy looked at her closely. There was only moonlight, and it was difficult for Irene to read his expression. "We did *that* to them," he said. "Isn't that enough?"

"She was so alone."

"She was the guardian of the threshold. They're always composed of opposites, you see." Glorian paused to ladle soup into a bowl for Irene. "She was alone, but she was in the middle of a great city. She was poor in material things, but there were legitimate means for satisfying her wants. Was she unhappy?"

"Unhappy?" asked Irene. She thought back. Happiness or unhappiness didn't seem to matter to the shopping-bag woman. "I don't know."

"Ambiguous," said Glorian. "Essential. Once you've passed that, you've left the last clinging bits of the useless Irene behind, in the shopping bags, in the waste receptacle, on the bench, on the subway tracks, in the pockets of the rushing commuters. You've passed the custodian of the way. When you entered her domain, all you saw was darkness beyond. But your spirit—*your* spirit, Irene—led you through. Now you are stronger. Would you like some oyster crackers in that?"

"Please," she said, her voice subdued. She couldn't help recalling the fear and the anguish she had felt, not just in the old woman's body, but also all around it, in the other people, the younger people, the rich and the poor. "I'm eighty-two years old, and I have done nothing with my life."

"I wouldn't say that, Miss Irene," said Glorian. "You've lived it, haven't you? For eighty-two years? That's as much as you can do with a life."

"Life is a cycle," she murmured. "Born, grow, live a few years, get old, die. A nice cycle. A perfect cycle. People like that old woman, they have their cycle interrupted. They can't enjoy it. I've had a perfect life, really, in a way. No worries, no madnesses that I haven't been able to take care of on my own. But the cycle..."

"Would you like to be young again?"

"What?" cried Irene, with a laugh. "In my own blue Cub Scout uniform?"

"No, I don't mean like me," said Glorian. "Do you have a desire to be young again?"

"Everyone does."

"Yes, I know. I don't understand it. They taught me that when I was just in training, and I've never grasped the importance of being young again. I like to keep on going."

Irene sighed in the growing darkness. "Glorian," she said softly, "*you* can just keep on going. *We* can't."

"Ah," said Glorian, "that might have something to do with it."

Chapter Five

The Surprise of a Lifetime

Irene felt like she was dreaming.

She had opened her eyes and she was still lying on the ground in the forest, and the birds cheeped above her, and a squirrel ran across the small clearing they had camped in, and everything else seemed the same. But she felt like she was dreaming.

How does one tell if one is awake or dreaming?

Irene sat up, and there were no aches or stabbing pains. Her whole body felt different than it ever had before. She looked at her hands. They were strong hands.

She looked at her arms. They were strong arms, strong forearms, heavily muscled upper arms.

She looked down at her body. Her chest was broad and deep. Her torso was trim, her stomach flat and strong. Her legs were the legs of an athlete. Her skin was dark, as if it had been many hours working under the sun.

Irene looked at her body. It was a young body. That was one of the reasons she felt like she was dreaming. She was in a young, healthy, strong, wonderful body.

It was also a young, strong, *male* body.

"Glorian?" she asked, and her voice was a firm baritone. It startled her. The sensory impressions were beginning to be processed by her confused brain, and the dissimilarity of these young male senses made her so lost and bewildered that she could do nothing except sit beneath a tree and call for help. "Glorian?"

"I won't be with you," said Glorian's voice. He was nowhere in sight.

"Glorian?" begged Irene. The entire idea of changing from an old person to a young one again was difficult enough to believe. But the idea of changing from a woman to a man...

"Glorian?"

Her eyes were clear. She could see things...

Details. The leaves, the grass, the raggedness of the trees.

She could hear. Instead of a mild mumble of sounds, she heard the sharp, crisp snapping of twigs beneath her as she moved.

The air smelled beautiful. She took deep breaths, loving the clean smell, the fragrances she had not smelled since her own youth, fragrances she had forgotten.

And the body was strong. She stood up and she was awed by the way the arms and legs moved and worked, without effort. She walked around the campsite. She bent down-no knife of pain!— and picked up a long branch as thick as her new arm. She broke the branch and she laughed.

Then there was something else. The sense of maleness. It was there, behind the senses, lurking in the mind, always present somewhere but rarely coming out directly in her thoughts. It was unsettling. "This is what it's like to be a man?" she thought. The subtle feeling of agitation that accompanied her thoughts would not go away, she knew. "This is how a man thinks? This is why they act the way they do?" She was getting a little used to being a young man, but the oddness of it hadn't diminished.

She felt like she was dreaming. "People don't change like this," she thought.

A voice came to her through the air, the bright, morning woodland air. "It happens all the time." It was Glorian's voice.

"You come out here, Glorian."

"I can't, Irene. You may be right. It may be a dream."

"Glorian, I'm young, and I like it. But I'm a young man, and I *don't* like that at all. Now fix it."

"People change sexes all the time. There's all kinds of literary precedent. Ovid wrote about it. Virginia Woolf. Lots more."

"In the first place," said Irene, "I'm old—"

"No, you're not."

"And I'm a woman."

"No. Not anymore. Or maybe yes, if you're dreaming."

Irene broke another branch and threw the pieces. She liked the feeling of being able to throw. "Glorian?"

There was no answer.

She would go on. If she were dreaming, it didn't matter. If she weren't dreaming it wouldn't matter, either, because she would be dead soon—

—because she was an eighty-two-year-old woman. No, she wasn't. She was a young man, about twenty-six years old with short brown hair that was cut long in the front. She felt her face; she had no beard. She was dressed in a rough woolen tunic over a pair of trouserlike hose, and she had leather slippers that didn't fit very well.

Irene sat down to plan what to do next. She sat beside the dying fire of the night before. She scattered the embers with a stick, and covered them over with moist dirt. She was careful with her fires. Glorian had told her about that.

Glorian. Where was he? Irene looked around the clearing but there was no sign of him yet. But she did see a strange sparkle, an odd, pure gleam of bright golden light, like a jewel in a crown. It came from a place among the twisted roots of a huge tree. The sun was catching the face of something and beaming directly at her. She jumped up. She jumped up! It was incredible! She could jump again.

She went to the tree and looked at the object. It was a piece of twentieth-century Depression glass, a yellow Cloverleaf sugar bowl. "I'm dreaming," she thought. She took the sugar bowl and packed it in one of the bags. Then she walked around some more. She felt the peculiar male anxiety grow in her thoughts, then recede, then grow again. After a while she decided to go on without Glorian.

She wasn't an eighty-two-year-old woman anymore. She was a man. She *could* go on without him.

As she walked along she considered the whole matter of her journey and the ways Glorian was affecting it. Irene wanted control over her life, and that was one of the main reasons she had left the house of Michael and Constance. But even now, on the liberating expedition itself, someone else was presuming to dictate to her. It was a situation that depended on point of view. Irene *wanted* to go to California. Glorian told her that she *had* to. She had no regrets at leaving people and experiences behind. There would always be more. But Glorian was insisting that she welcome only the people and experiences he thought were right, and forcing on her things she never would have chosen for herself. She never would have chosen to become a shopping-bag lady. She never would have chosen to become a young man.

"Sure," said Glorian, who was about a step and a half behind her. "You love being a young man, don't you?"

Irene bit her lip to prevent herself from speaking. Then she remembered that apparently Glorian knew what she was thinking.

"Sometimes," he said.

Irene turned around. She was startled. He was another person again. "I wish you'd stop changing," she said.

Glorian laughed. "You're a fine one to talk," he said. He laughed some more. Irene didn't laugh. Glorian was shorter and older than the young man in the white robe he had been. He was wearing a woolen tunic and hose, like Irene's. He was shorter than Irene but broader in the shoulders, and he appeared to be stronger and heavier. He had dark hair and eyes. He wore a dandelion, which he had poked through his tunic. He had a ring on one finger, with a polished piece of alabaster set in it. "Come on, we've got to keep moving. I want to get out of here. I want to get out of this forest."

"I want to get out of this body," said Irene.

Glorian was surprised. "You prefer your old one?" he asked.

"No," she said, "not really. But if you're going to go on changing me into someone else, why don't you let me help pick out the body?"

"Sorry," said Glorian, "but you'll have to stay that way all through the next adventure. It's your first real trial. It's going to be a million times tougher than your initiation, and I have a lot to teach you. I want to get out of this forest, though. You see, I have changed because you have changed. I don't mean because you have changed bodily. I mean that you've passed your initiation. You are a different person, and I am a different person. Now I prefer low, level fields to forests."

"Does it matter what I prefer?" asked Irene.

"Not as much, because you don't know where we're going, and I do."

"Where are we going?" she asked.

"I can't give you that information, and you ought to know that. But there is a treasure to be defended. Great treasure."

Irene stopped and looked at Glorian. He had thick lips, a sloping forehead, and his eyes were too close together. Irene shuddered. "A treasure," she said. "You mean my soul, don't you?"

"No," said Glorian, "just a treasure. Money. That's why I look like this, and why I want to keep going, and why I don't feel like standing around all day talking. Let's get started. We'll cross the stream up there, and it's just a day's march through the forest until we get to the fields."

The feeling of being male and young rushed through Irene's body. Her mind felt swept away by it. It stopped her from answering, and before she could speak, Glorian had walked on ahead. She followed. She was getting to enjoy her new body. She no longer felt like she was dreaming.

About noon the two young men stopped for something to eat. While Irene gathered berries and fruit, Glorian put together another table. When Irene came back she saw that Glorian had become a Cub Scout again. She refused to say anything. She refused to let Glorian shock or surprise her anymore. At least, anymore that day.

"Look, Miss Irene!" said the boy, who was a little different. He was a little larger and older than he had been. "I've got my Bear Badge, now. I'm really on my way!"

"You'll be an Eagle Scout before we get to California," she said.

"Oh, sure," said the boy, Glorian, "it's just like I told you. It's taken for granted."

"I found some fruit and berries. The forest is a good provider."

"I made lunch. Hamburgers, rolls, pickle relish, catsup, I forgot mustard, and potato chips. And bug juice to drink."

"Bug juice?"

Glorian laughed. "That's what we always call it."

After lunch they began walking again. Glorian changed from his nine-year-old identity back into his more bull-like, persistent self. They walked through the woods, and Irene was glad that they would soon be out of the forest. She, too, was weary of the way they had come, and welcomed the thought of a different scene. "Glorian," she said, "you told me I'm going to have this adventure soon."

"Yes," he said. "Not today. Not tomorrow. Leave it that way."

"The day after tomorrow?"

"Maybe."

"You're getting laconic, aren't you?"

Glorian shrugged his massive shoulders. "It's part of this Taurus personality. I can't help it. I'm sorry."

"Well," said Irene, who felt so good that she wanted to run on ahead, "it might be a good idea if you tried to prepare me for what I'll have to face."

"Can't you let it rest for even one day?" asked Glorian moodily. "Tomorrow will be different. Ask me tomorrow."

"What's tomorrow?"

"Tomorrow we'll be near the site of the adventure, and I'll be out of this personality and into one a bit more Gemini, you know. More energetic. A good teacher. Enthusiastic about things like that. Wait until tomorrow."

"If it's my first trial, I think—"

"Read this," said Glorian, handing a pamphlet to Irene. The pamphlet looked like the first one, but it was called *England in the Tenth Century*.

"How is this going to help?" she asked. "It must be at least the twenty-third century already."

Glorian grunted, but he didn't say anything else. He just kept walking. Irene looked through the pamphlet. It had small chapters briefly describing the conditions of the English people while they were being raided by the Danes. Irene wondered what it was supposed to prepare her for. But if Glorian could make her a shopping-bag lady in hell, he could make her a Dane raiding the English countryside as well. And he didn't have to make *her* a Dane. He would make *him*—Irene—a Dane. That would explain why Irene was now a young man. She would be given a test of her moral character. She would be a Dane, swooping down with other Danes on some unsuspecting English abbey, and Glorian would watch while everyone else was fighting and killing and laughing and sacking and pillaging. Glorian would observe Irene's behavior.

She wondered what her behavior ought to be. At first, she thought that she should hang back and not take part, showing that she did not condone the senseless slaughter and all the rest. But it occurred to her that she might be expected to take an active role, to prove that she could adapt well to changes and to changing systems of ethical behavior. Perhaps that evening, after they had stopped for the day, she could read the pamphlet more closely. She packed it in one of the bags and slung the bag over her shoulder.

"Glorian," she said, "I wonder if you'd mind discussing this whole affair with me. It's about time we got some things straight."

"Miss Irene," he said, stopping and facing her, "just because you suddenly find yourself in a strong man's body, don't think that you can pressure me with threats. Remember that for all the additional strength you have gained, you have come nowhere near the lower limits of my Knowledge or powers."

"All right, fine," she said. "I mean the business of my going to California. Looked at in the new light of my transformation. It's nice of you to make me more comfortable, and it makes our progress across country much quicker. But I don't see why you have to keep up the mystery. I think I'm entitled to some answers. What kind of trial do I have to face? What is this treasure I have to defend? What's this business about England in the tenth century."

"First," said Glorian, sighing, "there is such a thing as your composite myth. Your generalized-myth scenario. That's what we've drawn up for you. It goes like this. A hero or heroine receives a call to adventure. The call is answered or it is not. If it is answered, the hero or heroine starts on his or her way, and meets supernatural aid in one form or another. In this case, it's me. Sometimes it's a good witch or some ridiculous talking animal. The hero or heroine crosses the threshold and loses some of himself and gains something more valuable. Then there are a string of trials or labors, and when they are completed the hero or heroine is greatly rewarded. He or she then returns home to share the reward."

"Why should I share anything with them?" asked Irene.

"Because by then you'll be noble."

"Ah," said Irene doubtfully.

"Second," said Glorian, "your first trial will occur in England in the tenth century."

"I gathered that."

"It is the first step on the road to your goal, to the gateway of the new light."

"I don't want a gateway to the new light," she said. "Just the butter dish and a quick trip home. My old age, my condition, my real condition"—she hit her broad chest—"has led me to change from a life of wishing to a life of hoping. I've changed from material things to spiritual things. That's what getting old means. I am what I was, plus what I am. To you, there is only a surface, the current moment as a preparation for something you have picked out for me."

"Spiritual things?" he asked. "What about the butter-dish top?"

"My life is complete," she said. "Beautifully complete. I have no wordly wishes, except a quiet and dignified ending, and the top to the stupid butter dish. Why don't you make me one?"

"I can't," said Glorian.

"What about the sugar bowl I found?"

"I didn't make that," he said. He sounded worried. "You found a sugar bowl?"

"Yes," said Irene. She unpacked it and showed it to him.

"This could mean danger," he said.

"Then maybe we should go home."

Glorian looked at the young man whose frame housed Irene's identity. After a few seconds, Irene laughed. "Come on," she said.

"I wish I could make you see the true importance of this journey," said Glorian. "It would make things easier, it would make the trials less dangerous, it wouldn't tax me nearly as much. You have no idea how tiring it gets changing back and forth, back and forth, from one body to another, over and over again. I don't need the aggravation."

"Then don't do it."

"I have to. It's part of the job. I have a contract."

Later in the evening the two young men agreed to have their supper. Glorian went into the woods a little, excusing himself, and when he returned he was a Cub Scout again. "I'm working on my activity badges to become a Webelos Scout," he said. "It's more difficult. It's tougher these days."

"I can imagine," she said. Irene, in her male body, looked like Glorian's older brother. She couldn't help feeling protective toward him. She wondered if he felt awkward about the situation.

"Yes," he said.

"How did you know I was thinking that?" she asked.

"I am Glorian of the Knowledge. I have my ways. I have the Knowledge of the working of the things."

"And you have braces on your teeth."

Glorian frowned. "They'll be off before I make Webelos. You have to earn these activity badges, and I'm working on Naturalist. I have to do four out of seven requirements. One of them, though, is to visit a museum of natural history or a zoo. There aren't any, anymore."

"I see your problem. We could eat."

"Why don't you go see if you can find any wild greens for a salad," he said. "I'll have everything else done."

"That's not fair, Glorian," said Irene. "Let me help."

"Go," said Glorian. Irene went, but she was hurt. She spent some time in the woods thinking of ways to get back at Glorian, but after half an hour, when she heard him calling, she went back to their campsite. "I thought you got lost," he said.

"You hurt my feelings," said Irene. "You're too preoccupied with this quest of yours. You're showing no sympathy for my feelings at all. Here I am in a strange body, and you leave me to adjust to it, as if it were nothing. I have some kind of trial coming up, and you're too busy to help. And I want to contribute! I want to do something, but your Knowledge has made you too proud to accept a poor old woman's help. I'm sorry, Glorian, but you are not a person, a human being, and you can't expect to treat me like this without hurting me."

Glorian was ashamed. His young face blushed red and he looked at the ground. He was cleaning sticks and whittling points on them to toast marshmallows after dinner. Irene saw that he was crying. "I'm sorry, Miss Irene," he said. "You're right."

Irene was so sorry she had spoken; she had no idea that Glorian would take it to heart. "It's all right, Glorian," she said.

"No. I'm humiliated. I've failed."

"Glorian, listen to me. You just have to remember that I have a part in this thing, too, whatever it is, and that I deserve to know some of the details. I have enough trouble managing this enormous body without walking cold into centuries I've never seen before."

"Forgive me, Miss Irene. And sign this, please."

She took the paper and pen from him, signed it, and gave it back. He put them away somewhere. He wouldn't look at her. He was still a nine year-old boy, crying.

"What's for supper?" Irene asked.

"Hot dogs," said Glorian, in better spirits. "And baked potatoes that will be burned on the outside and raw in the middle."

"Wonderful," said Irene. There was no table this time, so the two young men sat down to eat supper on the grass.

Afterward, Glorian came closer to Irene's side and put a hand on her shoulder. "I suppose you're right," he said. "I should let you know more about what you're going to face. Let's take a look at the pamphlet, and I'll run through it with you. Then you'll know which is the important stuff and which is the material you can just forget."

"Before you do that, Glorian, would you mind changing back? It's hard for me to listen to you lecture when you're such a dear little boy."

"Oh, good grief," said Glorian. He stood up. "Bank the coals," he said. Irene went to the remains of their cooking fire and did as he said. When she turned around, he was a different Glorian again. "After midnight I'm supposed to look like this," he said. "I took the liberty of changing a bit early. It won't do any damage, and this form is a good deal better suited to helping you through the rough spots." He was much taller than he had been, with long, thin arms, and he was dressed in a light violet robe. He had a silver band around his long brown hair, and there was a single beryl set in it, over his forehead.

"Very impressive, Glorian," said Irene. "I heartily approve. A decided change for the better."

"Forget that. Napoleon once said that he felt himself driven toward an end, some end, something he couldn't really foresee. But he had the feeling that as soon as he reached this unguessable ending, whatever it was, the tiniest thing, a breath or a feather, would be enough to break him. But he made the point that until that day, until the day of his spectacular ending, nothing in the world could stand in his way. We have to get you thinking like that. We have to improve your own self-image. We have to get you thinking in terms of this quest as a whole, rather than going so many miles today and stopping, and going so many miles tomorrow. What does it all mean?"

"You're asking me?" said Irene. "That's out of character."

"Do you feel impelled? Do you feel that nothing stands in the way of your progress? That nothing can harm you until you've achieved your goal?"

"I don't feel that way at all," she said. "Just this afternoon I nearly tore my left arm off in a briar bush."

"But you have to feel that way, Miss Irene. You have to see this as an unstoppable progression of exploits, leading you from one height to another, until you grasp whatever it is you want to grasp."

"The butter dish," she said.

"Eternal glory might be better," he said. "Or the admiration of all people down through eternity."

"My butter dish."

"The Manifest Destiny of Miss Irene!" cried Glorian.

"The pamphlet, and the old one, and your conversation keep using words I don't understand," said Irene. "I wish you'd clear them up for me."

"Certainly," said Glorian. He was enthusiastic. He stood up and paced back and forth in front of her. He cleared his throat. "Definition of terms. A grand way to begin. Proper. Yes. Well. A country is made up of states, and a state is made up of cities, and a city is made up of a concentration of people all living nearby."

"Like the house of Michael and Constance."

"No," said Glorian. "A city would have, oh, maybe a hundred thousand houses like that, and a state would have dozens of cities, and half a hundred states would make a country."

"There couldn't be that many people," said Irene. "It's foolish."

"There could be that many people if people were really serious about it and paid attention to their duties and obligations."

"That's enough, Glorian," said Irene. "I didn't marry, and I didn't have children, and I'm not sorry."

"Never mind that, then. The world is flat, surrounded by a blue vault that we call the sky or the heavens. The sun and moon are large, but they look small because they're so far away. Does that make sense?"

"Yes," said Irene, "so far."

"Good," said Glorian. "The sun and moon are the same size, about thirty-six miles in diameter, and about three thousand miles above our heads."

"Three thousand miles!" said Irene. "It makes me queasy just to think of the sky being that far away. All that empty space."

"It's the way that the Powers That Be designed the universe. It serves their purposes, and we must make our own purposes fit harmoniously within their framework."

"And that's the universe? I'd like for you to explain to me how it works," she said. "Before we get to California. I recall that when I was a young girl someone taught me these things, but I seem to remember the distances as being somewhat larger."

"A common error," said Glorian. "A mistake made by people too close-minded to accept the truth when it is shown to them. The Knowledge."

"I am always open to new thought," said Irene.

She washed and repacked the few things she had taken from her bags, and Glorian had made the remainder of their meal, the garbage and the melted marshmallow middles, disappear by whatever private disposal service he had. Irene put one bag beneath a tree, and the other bag beneath a second tree, as pillows. It was getting late, and the day spent as a young man had been tiring. They had pushed themselves, and they had marched a long distance. Irene felt fatigued, but pleasantly so, and she felt vibrant. She felt young. She saw that Glorian had put the blanket by her bag. "Thank you, Glorian," she said. "Are you sure you don't want it, tonight? I'm dressed more warmly than you."

"Thank you, Miss Irene, but no. It would be a mark of dishonor if I were to take your blanket."

"What if I give it to you?"

"You can't give it to me."

Irene was furious. "There you go again!" she shouted. "Telling me I *can't* do something. I've had to put up with a lot of punishment on this trip. My pride has been hurt more times in the last few days than in all the years I lived with Michael and Constance."

"That isn't true," said Glorian calmly. "I know how often they hurt you. Hurt your pride. Hurt your dignity."

"Yes," she said softly. She went to her sleeping place. She made ready to lie down. Beside her bag there was something that fell over in the leaves as she sat down. She reached out and picked up the object. It was another piece of Depression glass, a three-legged pink Swirl candy dish. "Glorian," she called.

"Yes?"

"Glass here. A piece of Depression glass."

He hurried over to her side. He took the candy dish and examined it. "Those fiends," he muttered. "Those animals."

"What's wrong?"

Glorian looked up and took a deep breath. He paused. "Oh, nothing, Miss Irene," he said. "You have opposition. Your first trial begins and finishes the day after tomorrow. It may be more difficult than I thought."

"Can I keep the Depression glass?" she asked.

Glorian sighed. "Yes," he said, "I guess it doesn't make any difference now."

Irene was happy. She packed the candy dish carefully. She was on the ground, staring up at the tree, its boughs and leaves sheltering her, the stars like points of ice in the black sky sometimes visible when the branches moved. Her new body began to feel restless, and the feeling made Irene uneasy. She didn't know how to interpret the feeling. It was a purely male feeling, and she knew that there might be other purely male feelings that she would discover. She had a difficult time falling asleep. Just before she did, she thought that Glorian knelt beside her and spoke with her. She couldn't recall any of the words or even the subject of their discussion, but she had the feeling that she had gained a valuable insight, an important, an all-important, vital, life-saving insight. But before she fell deeply asleep she had forgotten it, and in the morning, she knew there would only be the feeling of having lost something irreplaceable. That's the way it was every morning, whether she was male or female.

Chapter Six

Serfs Up!

"Good morning, Miss Irene!"

Irene opened her eyes slowly. She was beginning to detest the way Glorian woke her every morning. She liked to sleep. She had always thought that sleep was a fine thing, a genuinely good force in the universe. She was a champion sleeper. When she slept, she put her heart into it. That was why Glorian's early-morning exhortations annoyed her.

"Get up, Miss Irene!" said Glorian. He looked the same as the evening before, violet robe, silver circlet. "Rise and shine!"

"I'll rise," Irene muttered, "but I'll be damned if I'm going to shine." She threw off the blanket and screamed. She was in the body of a young man! She thought that had all been a dream.

"If that had been a dream," said Glorian, trying to be reasonable, "what would that have made the dreams you had last night?"

"What dreams?" asked Irene, standing and stretching. "You mean when I thought that you told me something important?"

"No, that was no dream. The dream was that you were back in school, and it was after the Christmas vacation, and you couldn't find your locker, and you couldn't remember your lock's combination, and you were in the junior-class play that night and hadn't learned any of your lines, and you were naked."

Irene gazed at Glorian and shook her head. "This Knowledge of yours is some powerful thing," she said.

"I know," said Glorian. He smiled. He was very proud.

They decided to skip breakfast and get right to the day's march. They packed quickly, and Glorian took the lead. "It's only a little farther before we leave this forest," he said. "Then it's mostly meadows and open fields all the way." As he spoke, his long violet robe was snagged on a bush. Irene saw him say something under his breath and wished that she could have heard it. He tugged at the robe for a while, then gave up. "Would you mind turning around for a moment?" he asked.

"Modesty?" said Irene, amused.

"No," said Glorian, "blinding flash of light."

Irene turned around and there was a great burst of light. She was startled. "All right," called Glorian, "you can turn around again." She did, and he was dressed like she was, woolen tunic and hose. His tunic had a hood, which he wasn't wearing up. They didn't say anything more to each other, but walked about twenty yards through the woods. Then, suddenly, they were on the edge of a wide meadow.

"Look at that!" said Irene.

"Nice, nice," said Glorian. "Flowers and things."

"Now where?"

"Straight across. We'll be where we're going by lunchtime, if we take the short route."

"Why would we ever take the long route?" she asked.

"Oh," said Glorian, "because"—he sneezed—"because there's an extra peril on the way, in case I need one." He sneezed again.

"Hay fever," said Irene. "I'm glad we don't need an extra peril."

"After showing me that glass yesterday, I'm sure we'll have more on our hands than I had expected."

"How do you mean that?" she asked, as they started across the meadow.

Glorian sneezed twice before answering. "No time for that now," he said, winking at the author and reader. "It's more important that you study the pamphlet. It's urgent." They stopped and found it in one of the bags. *England in the Tenth Century.*

Irene found walking through tall grass and weeds while reading a little hazardous. She almost fell several times, but the material in the booklet was important enough to keep her reading. "How much of this is important?" she asked. "You never did get around to telling me."

Glorian stopped walking and thought. "Well, I thought you might not need it at all, really, except to prepare you for the cultural derangement. But that sugar bowl bothers me. So read the first part, about the Vikings. And that candy dish, that horrible candy dish. You'll have to read the section leading up to the end of the century. What part is that? Six?"

"Seven," she said.

"All right. Read Part One and skip to Part Seven. That will prepare you for the rest of the day. Then tonight I'll give you a pamphlet that goes into great, gory, awful detail about what you're going to see tomorrow."

"I don't like the way that sounds," said Irene.

"Let's get"—Glorian sneezed—"going."

Irene read the pamphlet. She stumbled over clods of earth and stones, but she knew that she was reading for her life. "About the year 800, Vikings came to raid England," she read. "They continued this raiding for about fifty years, coming in the spring, going home in autumn. Soon after the middle of the century they established bases along the coast of England. The English had given up seafaring before this time and there is no evidence that any English king of the time had a navy."

"Glorian," she said, "what's the difference between a Viking and a Dane?"

"No difference," he said. He sneezed. "Never mind. It's not important for our purposes where they come from."

"There must be a difference," thought Irene. If she were going to be a bloodthirsty Dane, that was one thing. But if she were going to be a proud Viking, rowing manfully in a Viking ship, with shields and swords and manful things, that would be thrilling!

She read on. "The Vikings first attacked monasteries. The invaders were probably surprised at finding these isolated communities, which were relatively wealthy and yet had no guards or defending forces. And, too, the monasteries were located along the coast, a perfect place for the Vikings, in order to isolate the monks even more from the world."

"How's it going?" asked Glorian.

"Am I going to have a test?" said Irene.

"Not from me," said Glorian. "From the keen edge of a battle-ax."

Irene stopped and stared. Glorian went on across the meadow. Irene turned to Part Seven. "In the latter part of the ninth century, an army of invading Danes landed in England. It roamed up and down the coast attacking towns and generally doing what one thinks the Danes and Vikings did. The army split about the year 876, half settling in southwest England, the other half scattered along the coastline. Nearly a century later, in 973, Edgar was crowned the first King of all England. Two kings later Aethelred Unred came to power. Unred means "bad counsel" or "poor planner," but he will always be known by the mistranslation of Aethelred the Unready. His reign marked a new era of corruption and indecision."

"Got it all?"

"That's it, Glorian," said Irene. "I'm finished reading."

Glorian laughed. "Fine," he said, "because here's the village."

Irene looked up and saw a row of timbered huts, arranged in two parallel rows. There were about twelve in all. Men and women were busily at their tenth-century chores all around them. Irene turned and looked back at the way they had come. There were fields cultivated with various crops, and men, women, and children working. "Where did this village come from?" she asked. "We didn't walk through those fields."

Glorian only shrugged.

"We're here, then," said Irene. "What a terrible-looking place. And the stench."

"It's genuine," said Glorian. "It's real. It's human. It's what life is like, under the shiny surface people like Michael and Constance put on it."

"I'm rather fond of the shiny surface myself," she said. In the fields, the autumn crops were being harvested. There were strips of land with maturing wheat, rye, barley, oats, peas, and beans. She stared at the fields, thinking. Something bothered her, but she couldn't quite get at it.

"It's late summer, early autumn," said Glorian.

"Right!" said Irene. "That's it. It wasn't, yesterday. Why?"

"Because the Battle of Maldon was fought on about August 10, according to most historians. That's tomorrow."

"Oh."

"You don't sound excited," said Glorian.

"I'm not," said Irene. It wouldn't be very much fun to come ravaging across the fields and lay waste to the tiny village. It wouldn't take very much to lay it to waste. One man with a hefty club could do it in an afternoon. But Glorian had mentioned a treasure. Financial, pecuniary treasure. Wealth. Capital. Assets. In this village? Not likely. Maybe the King's payroll was going to pass by on a messenger or something.

"Don't worry about it," he told her. "The pamphlet I'll give you tonight will put everything straight, in black and white. It will be a breeze tomorrow."

Irene noticed that someone was walking toward them, from one of the fields. He had been overseeing two youths plowing a fallow field. "Why are they plowing at harvest time?" she asked.

"Don't worry about it," said Glorian.

"Stop saying that and answer me."

"Because they're getting ready to sow the winter wheat and rye. And this man is the mayor of this tidy metropolis, so start fitting in. Just follow my lead."

Irene was suddenly terror-stricken. She felt her legs go weak, and she heard the blood pounding in her head.

"Who are you?" asked the man, the mayor of the village.

"You remember me, don't you, Grohthelm?"

The man looked closer at Glorian. "Ah, yes, my friend!" he said. "It's good to have you back. And this man is your companion?"

"Yes," said Glorian.

Grohthelm looked closely at Irene. She was still immobile with fear. She was afraid that Grohthelm would see through her, realize that beneath the brawny exterior there was an eighty-two-year-old woman and a trespasser in his century. "You don't look like a Viking," said the mayor. It was supposed to be a joke.

Irene didn't know that. "Well," she said, "I, uh, I'm from very far away, but—" Glorian poked her and she stopped. Glorian sneezed.

"You're probably some kind of enemy," said Grohthelm, "and I ought to slit your throat, but then I'd have every avenging army in the heathen world on my head, and me with a beautiful fourteen-year-old virgin daughter, guaranteed virgin, who'd make you a great wife with a little patience on your part."

"I see," said Irene. Most of her fear had gone away. It was quickly replaced by repugnance. "You certainly have a lovely village here," she said.

"We plan to keep it that way," said Grohthelm. "But our great earl decided not to give the Vikings their payoff, and now I'm hearing stories that we're in for a fight."

"You're in for a fight," said Glorian.

"Well," said the mayor, pounding Irene's chest, "I'm glad you two happened by. Unless you think you can get out of this fight, somehow."

"That was Byrhtnoth's job," said Glorian. "He should have paid them off."

Grohthelm grunted. He looked at Irene. "It's a bad time, lad, and it's the duty of every man to defend the land of the King and Church. You've never seen battle, have you? Soon the spear or pike will be the dearest friend you ever had, and the byrnie as sweet as any woman."

The mayor was about to go off to superintend someone else's work. Glorian caught him by the arm. "Do you know where we could stay the night?" he asked.

Grohthelm looked at Glorian with a frown. He thought for a long time. "Are you two going to be in the fight, then?" he asked.

"Certainly," said Glorian.

"Then you will stay with me."

"Thank you, Grohthelm," said Glorian. He turned to Irene.

"Oh," she said, "yes, thank you very much, sir." Grohthelm walked away and Irene felt the beginning of great fear rise in her. If the mayor had asked her, she knew that she couldn't lie convincingly. How could she stay in this wretched village, knowing that the next day she would return as a Viking to destroy it?

"You did well," said Glorian.

"I'm scared," said Irene.

"You did well."

"Glorian," she asked, "what's a byrnie?"

Glorian chewed his lower lip as he thought. "I don't know," he said.

"Some Knowledge," said Irene.

Glorian was offended. "Look," he said, "I have the Knowledge of the working of things. You find out what it is, and I'll tell you how it works." He sneezed.

"What do we do now?" asked Irene.

"Let's look around," said Glorian. "It would help you get used to being here, and among these"—he sneezed—"people."

"I want to get away from these huts," she said. "The smell is enough to make me sick."

"We'll walk in the fields, then." Glorian led the way down the single lane of the village. "Look," he said, "all around the huts are fields, large fields. There are about eight or ten fields. See?"

"Yes," said Irene. "Between the fields they have hedges or dirt banks. One field for every family?"

"No," said Glorian. "This is the beginning of feudalism. They work all the fields together. Each family has one strip in each field. Also the Church has a strip, and the earl has a strip, and the villagers have to work about three days a week for them. Already, the people are tied to the land. On top of that, they have to pay taxes out of what they grow on their own strips, so that what they eat, what goes on the table, is made up not so much from what grows in the fields, but what they're growing in small vegetable gardens around the huts."

"It's a horrible way to live," said Irene.

"Not too bad," said Glorian. "This system wasn't forced on them. It evolved. In return, they get the protection of the lords above them."

"Great protection," said Irene. "Like tomorrow? Against the Vikings? The protection is that they have to go out themselves and fight."

"Well," said Glorian, "I never said it was a perfect system."

"Their idea of agriculture isn't very advanced," said Irene, watching the boys plowing.

"One field is under cultivation, one field is being plowed and sown, and one lies fallow. They don't understand much about fertilizer, and they don't keep cattle, anyway, for manure. They have maybe one or two oxen in the whole village. Some wild hogs, tied up. They rarely eat meat, and then it's pork. And chickens. And beef, when an ox dies."

Glorian and Irene passed the afternoon walking in the fields. The crops that had matured looked poor. The villagers would not eat well that winter, especially after the abbey, the King's tax collector, the earl's tax collector, and Grohthelm took their shares.

It was already dusk when Glorian and Irene returned to Grohthelm's house. "House" it was by definition only. What it was actually was a hovel made partially of wood and mud and whatever else had been around. It was fairly roomy inside, but it was intended to house Grohthelm, his wife, Byrtha, one son, two daughters, a half-blind old man named Sigismund, who was the mayor's official retinue, and Grohthelm's mother. This was the largest house in the village, and beside the people, a small flock of chickens lived indoors as well. That was the local practice. "I don't believe it," said Irene.

"It will take the Norman Conquest to change things," said Glorian.

"Let's come back after that."

Glorian gave a short laugh. "Maybe we will," he said.

Grohthelm and his son had not come in from their work in the fields. Byrtha made Glorian and Irene comfortable on the floor, and they waited in the stifling hut, leaning against one wall.

"Huh," said Grohthelm when he came in. He said nothing else to anyone. He went to the pot where Byrtha had been making supper and got himself a bowl of porridge. There were some vegetables from the garden, too, probably because of the arrival of Glorian and Irene. Grohthelm was busy eating, but he signaled that they, too, should begin their supper.

The boy came in and got himself a bowl, and Byrtha filled one for her two daughters and herself. Grohthelm signed again that Glorian and Irene should eat, but there were no more bowls. Sigismund and Grohthelm's mother had to wait for someone to finish, and so would the two travelers.

While waiting, Irene nudged Glorian on the shoulder. "Listen," she whispered, "I really don't think I'm going to be able to take part in that fight tomorrow. It has me terrified. I may look like a young buck to you, but I'm an old woman. An old woman who has never had a fight in her life, let alone a battle, let alone a *real* battle with all kinds of sharp metal things trying to kill me."

"You'll do fine. Here's the pamphlet. Read it, and you'll see what I mean." He gave her another pamphlet. On the cover it said: Battles of No Significance Series. No. 991: *The Battle of Maldon.*

She opened it and began reading, knowing that what was in

the thin booklet was all that stood between her and a different kind of death than she had hoped for. She wondered at Glorian's confidence. "Close to the end of the tenth century," she read, "the climate of relations had changed. The Danes, or Vikings, were not returning each year to make raids. Rather, they were building fortifications. They weren't interested in making a living in England, as their colonizing predecessors had. These Vikings were professional soldiers, without women and children among them.

"The attacks on the monasteries had brought monastic life almost to an abrupt end along the eastern coast of England. Treaties between the English and the Viking raiders permitted some of these monasteries to be rebuilt. It became a popular joke of the time to cite the growing number of abbeys, each with its own relics of new and heretofore unheard-of saints. The monastic revival around Maldon began near the year 970."

Irene skimmed some of the next sections, dealing with local laws and their enforcement. She wanted to get to the battle itself. "The shire," she read, "was ruled by an ealdorman (or earl). One of the principle functions of the earl was to lead his men into battle whenever necessary. These earls were royal officials; later the office and title became hereditary. By using the earls, the King could keep in touch with all parts of his kingdom without being bothered with trivial problems."

"Doggone it," thought Irene, "I want the battle, blow by blow." She found the account of the battle near the end of the pamphlet. While the battle was of little or no historical significance, the discussion of that nonsignificance was more significant. There were only a few mentions of the battle in the contemporary histories, and but a fragment of a poem about it. The poem, one of the earliest in the English language, was deeply moving. Irene felt herself pitying the poor English villagers. The next day the earl, Byrhtnoth, who had refused to pay the Vikings' tribute, would lead the men of the shire of Essex into battle. He would face a fierce band of Vikings, who were camped across the mouth of the Blackwater River on an island. There was a ford, a kind of causeway, and the Vikings asked if they could be granted safe passage to the English side, where they would take up the battle.

Byrhtnoth, in a gesture more magnificent than wise, held his men back until all the Vikings had crossed. Then the Vikings began to cut the English down, every one of them, to the last man. A little note was made in the journal of the abbey at Ely concerning the battle, for the abbey was not far away and it enjoyed Byrhtnoth's favor while he was alive. The monks there took his headless body to the abbey for burial.

That was it. Vikings won, English zero.

Irene felt the same kind of confidence that Glorian had shown. He still refused to discuss the battle with her, but now she knew what to expect. Her sensitivity was the key, as she had proven during her initiation. She would be the poet, the inspired genius who would record the battle for history. Apart from the fighting, yet passionately involved.

Then, next, Irene felt an almost overpowering shock, a soul-deep pity for the people around her. Grohthelm would die the next day, along with his young son. And possibly old Sigismund, too. And all the male adults of the village. All the Essex levy. At harvest time, bereaved, the widows, the women...

"Why are you weeping?" asked Glorian.

"You must know," she said. "The fate of these people. What will happen to them?"

"They will go on, those who survive. They will work under immense burdens made heavier through the centuries. They will work and curse and make love and steal and revolt against excess. They will turn into Michael and Constance."

"Glorian," said Irene, "if you can't find a tear for these men, slain because their honor was too great for them to desert their fallen leader, then I think that whatever Michael and Constance are, they are in some ways better than you."

There was a brief suggestion of a smile. Then, gently, Glorian said, "Would they find the tears?"

"I'm sure they would."

"If they were among the Vikings?"

Irene hesitated. "I'm sure that tomorrow, some of the Viking soldiers will appreciate the honor and courage of the English."

"That is true. But there will be no tears, not there. There will be tears on the English side, you can be sure."

"It will be a horrible thing to see."

"More horrible than you can imagine," said Glorian.

"Would you care to eat now, my lads?" asked Grohthelm's wife, Byrtha. She held out a wooden bowl of porridge to Glorian. The bowl she handed to Irene was green glass, Depression glass, of a pattern called Colonial Rope.

"Lord," she whispered.

"It will be more horrible than you can imagine," murmured Glorian. He waited until the mayor's wife went away. He put his bowl on the floor. He looked at Irene. She was still staring in amazement at the glass bowl. "Irene," he said.

"Hm?"

"Irene, look at me."

She shook her head as though to clear it, and looked at Glorian. "Irene," he said in a soft voice, "do you know where you will be tomorrow?"

"I do," she said.

"You will not be among the Vikings."

"Yes, I know that."

"But you *will* be in the battle. *In* the battle."

She stared for a moment. "My God in heaven," she whispered. "Among the English?"

"Yes," said Glorian.

"But what kind of trial is that?" she asked hoarsely. "What kind of challenge is that? Everyone on the English side is killed. What does that prove about my moral character?"

"This might be more serious than I ever thought," said Glorian. "I've never had an initiate killed by doing the *correct* thing. What could it mean?"

"It means, Glorian, that I just won't go to the battle. I'll pass up on the battle, thank you, and continue my walk to California."

"Oh, Irene, Irene," said Glorian helplessly, "you're so bound up in this mystical matrix that you couldn't walk ten yards without being snared and vanished by something. I mean, look around here. It's the tenth century. Michael and Constance are gone forever. California may be available through some kind of transcendent sacrifice, though."

"Is California worth it?" she asked.

"You tell me. You're the one who wants to go there. A transcendent sacrifice. That's happened only two or three times in the whole history of the world! I never thought... I never *imagined* that *I'd* be called on to guide—"

"Forget it, Glorian," said Irene. "I'll sleep here tonight. Tomorrow, very early, I'm going to start walking due west, just the way I was going before I met you."

"You're not even a woman anymore," said Glorian. He sounded deeply agitated. "You're not you. You can't do that. A transcend—"

"I'll try," she said.

Glorian didn't answer.

"I'll need a new bag to carry all this glass," she said thoughtfully.

"Here," said Glorian. Now he sounded angry. He gave her a third bag. She spent some time rearranging her belongings.

"You're feeling lust, aren't you?" he asked. "For the fourteen-year-old daughter?"

"Lust? Is that what it is? Is that what male lust is like?"

"It can be a whole lot stronger. I can adjust it for you."

Suddenly Irene's eyes opened wider, and she gasped. She was in the grip of a compulsion more intense than anything she had ever felt before. "Stop," she whispered weakly. "Oh, dear Lord."

"If women understood," said Glorian. "If men understood."

"I don't understand why you did that, Glorian," she said.

"You'll never get to sleep, what with worrying about the battle, and the lust thing, and the new Depression glass, and what it all means. I can help you."

"Magic? Hypnotism?" asked Irene.

"Seconal," said Glorian. "Just one. I'll wake you early."

"*Very* early. I want to beat the rush, and I don't want to meet it coming the other way."

Soon she fell asleep, still leaning against the wall. Glorian moved her carefully so she would be sleeping more comfortably on the hard-packed dirt floor. He made certain that none of the others in the house was looking, and he kissed Irene's masculine cheek. Gently then, he said, "Good night, Irene." He sat back up against the wall and waited.

Chapter Seven

We All Make Mistakes

A foot kicked Irene's legs and woke her up. She sat up suddenly blinking her eyes. The kick was a change, not a particularly pleasant change, from Glorian's hearty "good mornings." She was about to say something when she realized that it hadn't been Glorian who had kicked her. It was Grohthelm.

"Up, fellow," said the man. "You'll learn a lot today. It's time to get started."

"What?" asked Irene.

"Good morning," said Glorian. He had appeared and sat down next to Irene.

"You were supposed to wake me early," she said.

"You two get ready," said Grohthelm, "I have other things to see to. I have to get this whole villageful of worthless bodies organized. I'll see you later. There's cold porridge, some ale, and a few onions left."

"You were supposed to wake me early," said Irene.

"You looked so comfortable asleep," he said. He smiled.

Irene was becoming angry. "Stop smiling," she said. "You didn't have any right to let me sleep. I told you to wake me, so that I could leave before what's-his-name and the others got up."

"Irene, you have to go through with it."

She shook her head. "I don't have to go through with anything. Now, I'm going to grab something to eat, and while the village is in a mild confusion I'm going to disappear through the fields. You can come with me if you like, but I don't care."

"Irene!" cried Glorian. "We went through this last night. You can't miss the battle. It's the first trial. Your quest to California. You have trials along the way. This is the first. If you run out now you'll never pass the test. You'll never get to California. Going through a trial and failing is better than avoiding a trial altogether. Please, listen to me."

Irene was very angry now. "What happens, then, if I do run away?"

Glorian took both of her hands and squeezed them. "Do you know what happened to the last initiate I led who tried to avoid a trial?"

"How could I?" said Irene brusquely.

"He was grabbed. He had his soul dried and minced and used as a herb."

Irene didn't say anything. She had never heard anything more absurd in her life. Being in the tenth century was the most absurd thing that had ever happened to her. Having to attend and take part in a slaughter was the most absurd—no, she thought, absurd wasn't the right word, particularly since she was going to be on the losing side. It wasn't absurd. It was just unnecessary.

"It *is* necessary," said Glorian. "If you go to the battle and die there, your name will resound through history. The last transcendent sacrifice became the center of a religious movement that ranked fifteenth in the world. And afterward there might be the chance to pass on to more spiritual adventures, and more spiritual trials, and I'll be with you every step of the way."

"All right," said Grohthelm, "let's go."

"Too late," said Glorian. "I guess we'll just have to make the best of it."

Irene glared at Glorian. "First opportunity," she said. She jerked a thumb over her shoulder.

"We're all ready here, sir," said Glorian. He helped gather together the three bags. He carried two and gave one to Irene.

Outside were the other men from the village. Most of the boys were there as well. Some didn't look more than twelve years old. Glorian and Irene took their places among them. "This is just awful, Glorian," whispered Irene.

Glorian nudged her. "You think this is bad," he whispered, "wait until you see the regular army."

The town's minutemen looked frightened and a little foolish. Irene knew just what kind of enemy they would be facing, and what kind of battle. But the men and boys were standing, talking, kicking stones back and forth, pretending they weren't too concerned. There was not a single ring of chain mail or a single sword among them. They looked, as they did every single day of their lives, like Anglo-Saxon peasants, churls, and serfs. Their armory consisted of knives, clubs, and pruning bills.

After a while, Grohthelm came to inspect them. "Line up," he said. "Regular lines. Straighten them up. The earl is going to look you over later, you know, and I don't want any of my people embarrassing me in front of the earl."

"You ever seen the earl?" asked one of the boys.

"Seen him?" said Grohthelm. "Seen him? I want to tell you, boy, I've seen him. I've eaten with him, drunk ale with him, watched him make rich land-owners run into little puddles of men, and I've had him call me by name, on three separate occasions. Next to the King, Byrhtnoth is the greatest man in England."

"He is the greatest," said one of the men.

"When you remember who the King is," said another. There was laughter.

"Shut up," said Grohthelm. "We're going to be fighting today for Aethelred. You forget how Unready he's been, and look to your own selves. Right? Now, straighten up. Space it out. I want a head count."

It took a while for an accurate count to be taken, and after that there wasn't much to do except wait. They would be joined by the levy of men from neighboring villages, and that horde of pitiable soldiers would arrive soon.

"I don't have a weapon," called Glorian.

Irene elbowed him in the stomach. "Don't attract attention," she said. "It's bad enough as it is it. I can't take off across the fields while we're waiting here in these lines."

Grohthelm walked over to Glorian. "That's right," said the mayor. "You and your friend. I'm sorry you have to get mixed up in this, but it's just bad luck and the Lord has reasons. Clodo, get these two men something to fight with."

Clodo, the serf, didn't know where to find weapons. The villagers themselves didn't have enough to go around, let alone lend to two strangers. Clodo solved the problem by bringing two lengths of heavy tree branch, each about thirty inches long. "Good," said Grohthelm. "Good clubs. Mash the filthy Viking heads. Swing 'em a good one in the face, and they'll respect Aethelred, and Byrhtnoth, and Grohthelm."

"No, they won't," said Irene softly. When Grohthelm walked away, Irene hefted her club. "You know what's bad about a club?" she said.

"No," said Glorian, "you can easily kill someone with that."

"I'll tell you," she said, "and remember that I'm an old woman, and you're the one with the Knowledge. In order to kill someone with this, they have to be within thirty inches of me. And before they get that close, their presence will be announced by a long spear, or an arrow, or a broadsword, or a pike, or a—"

"I found out what a byrnie is," said Glorian.

"Oh?"

"Yes," he said. "It's a corselet."

"What's that?"

"I don't know," said Glorian.

"Well," said Irene, smiling, "I do. It's a kind of body armor. A breastplate or chain mail."

Glorian smiled, too. "Good," he said. "Would you like to know how it's used?"

Irene sighed. "I can figure that out, myself," she said. "And, anyway, there aren't any."

"That's not my fault," said Glorian. "Don't blame me."

"Blankets you can find me. Dishes and marshmallows and extra knapsacks. Why don't you get me a good sword and some armor?"

"That's beyond my power," said Glorian complacently. "I wouldn't, even if I could. It would be interfering with your trial."

"Forget the sword," said Irene. "An armored vehicle of some sort." Glorian didn't bother to reply.

More than an hour later, the men from the neighboring villages approached them across the fields. They looked like a huge crowd until they got nearer. Then Irene saw that they weren't so many, and that they all looked exactly like Clodo, that they weren't armed any better, and they weren't marching with any kind of discipline, that none of them, including their nominal leaders, had had any kind of training for battle, and that they could not possibly, in any way except by divine miracle, be prepared to face an army of professional soldiers.

"Here they come," said Clodo, long after everyone else in the village had realized that fact for himself.

"Grohthelm!" called out an old man from among the new arrivals.

"Right," said Grohthelm. He went out to meet the man. The old man was evidently the leader of the party, and was giving instructions to Grohthelm. After a moment the mayor returned. "All right, I want you all to listen," he shouted. "We're leaving now. We're leaving now and we'll be joining the main army about four miles from here, at the crossroad. Remember that whatever happens, you're representing me on that battlefield, and you're representing our village. You don't want to make our village look bad, do you?"

"No," said three or four men.

"You don't want to make Byrhtnoth look bad, do you?"

No one said anything.

"Then the King," cried Grohthelm. "The King of all England!"

There was silence, except for the weeping of the town's women.

"All right," said the mayor, "forget it. But if you let the army down, if you turn coward, if you let those heathen Vikings whip you today, tonight they'll be here and you won't. Right here. In these houses. And they won't be thinking about getting out early in the morning to work in the fields. Figure that out for yourselves. Now line up with the rest of the levy and try not to hurt yourselves on the way." The villagers walked toward the men from the neighboring villages, and a few greetings were called out, but for the most part the mood was somber.

"They're all going to die," said Irene.

"Yes," said Glorian, "all of them. Except for the ones who desert. A few will desert. It's in the poem, there's always a few. And they'll live and come home. But all the rest..."

They walked across a couple of fields until they reached a narrow, rutted road. This road had been built by the Romans centuries before. Some of the roads in England had been built, others were mere tracks created by traffic over a period of time. The Roman roads had drainage ditches on both sides. Irene kept looking for an opportunity to lose herself, but nothing promising occurred. She couldn't bend over to tie a shoelace, because there weren't any on her slippers. The fields on either side were open, and she couldn't run across them without being seen by the army and recognized as a deserter. The penalty for that, after she was caught, would likely be death.

Then she had an inspiration. "Oh," she said, "I have a pebble in my shoe." She bent down and waited until everyone behind her had passed. She was alone. Then she stood up and walked to the side of the road. She planned to jump into the ditch and hide, but she was dismayed to see that it was filled with stagnant, evil-smelling, black water. "Blech," she said.

"Come on," said Glorian, taking her by the arm. "Let's catch up." Irene said nothing, and they marched quickly to rejoin the levy.

After an hour's march they arrived at the crossroad, which was broader. It was evidently a major route of commercial traffic. A murder that occurred along one of these roads was considered an offense against the King, instead of just a regular, normal killing. The army of churls sat down and waited for Byrhtnoth and the rest of the Essex army to meet them.

They waited only about twenty minutes. "I don't like this," thought Irene. "Everything is just too right. Everything is going along too close to schedule."

"Line up," shouted several men. The serfs did the best they could to present themselves as an ordered body of men, ready to meet their earl and receive his commands. Irene and Glorian stood near the front, now, and they were among the first to catch sight of Byrhtnoth himself.

It was an impressive sight. He was mounted on a huge white horse, whose trappings were beautiful and bright. The man himself was the kind of figure that once seen was never forgotten. Byrhtnoth, the earl of the shire of Essex, whose power in that shire was exceeded only by that of Aethelred himself—and that was a matter of opinion—was a giant of a man. Tall, broad, sitting straight in his saddle, his first impression on Irene was that such a man could not lose a battle, that the poem had to be mistaken. Byrhtnoth was nearly seven feet tall and immensely strong, although he was old, nearly sixty-five. He had been a hero many times before. This was by no means his first encounter with the Vikings. Beside him rode members of his *heorthwerod*, an Old English word that referred to

Byrhtnoth's personal friends and allies, men who had fought beside him on these previous occasions.

The elderly leader of the villagers shouted to Byrhtnoth as the earl passed, and Byrhtnoth raised one hand slightly in recognition. That was all. The villagers watched as the entire Essex levy passed by, and then they joined up behind. There would be other contingents joining later on the road.

Byrhtnoth knew what to expect, as did the members of his household force. But the hundreds of serfs who followed on foot, all armed as poorly as the men of Grohthelm's village, were only dimly aware of what the situation meant. They had no idea of what would be expected of them, or the size of their enemy's forces, or that, very likely, they were going to die. For the most part, Irene guessed after listening to the chatter and idle gossip of the serfs, the men believed that the Viking army was small and that the sight of Byrhtnoth and his army would be enough to put the raiders to flight. She knew how wrong that was.

It was not far from the crossroad to a smaller road that followed the Blackwater to the sea. Irene was becoming desperate. Glorian was trying to be cheerful, but that just made matters worse for her. He kept talking about how she was apparently to become one of the world's greatest inspirational figures. She just wanted to go home.

Another group of men joined the army, and then another. Neither band improved the levy's chances against the Vikings. There were few real weapons. The men carried only the implements they used in the fields or in their trades, things that might be used to inflict injury on another, as long as the other person was looking somewhere else. No one but Byrhtnoth's household force and a very few others even had shields.

It was early afternoon when they reached the mouth of the river. They could see Northey Island, on which the Vikings had made camp. They could see the Vikings. They could see the Vikings' weapons.

"I was holding out this hope that the poem didn't know what it was talking about," said Irene.

"Not much chance," said Glorian.

"No chance," said Irene. Surrounded by the hordes of serfs

drafted to stand up against the Vikings, there was nowhere to hide, nowhere to run. Irene had a fleeting thought that she could wait until the battle started, find a place somewhere in the middle, then fall down and pretend that she was already dead. But she knew that she'd be trampled and crushed. She discarded that plan.

"You know," said Glorian, "for every Viking you kill, you could put a notch on your club, and then—"

"What do I put the notch on with?" asked Irene. "Do you see a sharp instrument anywhere near here?"

"That young man, right there," said Glorian, "he's got a—"

"Hey, Godric!" called the young man.

"Godric?" asked Irene.

The young man came up to her and clasped her hand. "Godric!" he said. "Where have you been?"

Irene looked at Glorian, but he only shrugged. "Oh," she said, wondering who the young man was and who he thought she was, "I've been away."

"Away where?" The young man put an arm around Irene's shoulders and started walking away from Glorian. Irene cast an anxious glance backward, but Glorian had disappeared.

"Where?" said Irene. "Oh. On a mission. A special, secret mission."

"Ah," said the young man. He was leading Irene right toward the place where Byrhtnoth's own soldiers were preparing their weapons and getting ready for the action. "Look," called the young man, "does anyone have something for Godric here? Godric, just drop that foolish club."

"Not surprising that a son of Odda would go to battle and forget his blade," said one of the men.

Another man, tall, hugely built like Byrhtnoth, dressed in leather and chain mail, brought a weapon. "Take this, Eadmaer," said the man. "I can spare it." He gave it to Irene. It was a scramasax, a long, broad, single-edged knife that had been fixed to a slender shaft.

"Thank you, sir," said Irene.

"Godric, Odda's son," said the giant. He frowned. "We were just talking about you and your brothers. We didn't expect to see you this close to the front. Here, take this as well." He handed Irene yet another piece of twentieth-century Depression glass. This was a pink cup; the pattern was Sharon. Irene didn't show any sign that she was startled. She packed the cup away in her bag, wondering what it meant.

The young man, Eadmaer, said, "Godric, come with us. It will be better at the front. Best opportunity. Byrhtnoth himself will see you fight, and the glory will be greater. I know, I know all about the reputation you have. So this will be the time to show your valor against these savages."

Irene didn't want to be Godric. She didn't want to be anyone but Irene. Suddenly it seemed like years since she *had* been Irene. And, too, the name Godric meant something to her. She had read the poem and the pamphlet the night before, and the name Godric had been in it, but she couldn't recall why. She thought to get the booklet out and study up on it, but it was in one of the bags Glorian had been carrying, and he was gone now... .

"Godric." The giant was addressing him.

"Yes, sir," said Irene weakly.

"You will fight with us. Eadmaer told me. I am proud of you. Your father, Odda, would be proud. Come, sit with us until the work begins. We have some time."

Irene knew that she was going to be in very strong company. Eadmaer made a few introductions. Whoever Godric had been, he had known some of the important men and not known others. Irene met Wulfstan, a name that was also familiar. Part of her confusion was that in the poem almost everyone had names that were very much like.

"You remember Wulfmaer," said Eadmaer. "Wulfstan's son. And this is Aelfwine." He indicated another young man. The two glanced up and nodded. They were not overly pleased to see Godric. They were attired better than the villagers, far better, with short tunics beneath shirts of chain mail, conical helmets of iron bands, forged swords at their sides, and spears.

Irene glanced around. "Does anyone here have an extra shirt of mail?" she asked. There was a laugh from Wulfmaer.

Irene sat with them and listened to their conversation. The men of the household force were almost carefree, as though they had nothing more to do that afternoon than a little chore, a cleaning-up of some irritating pests. And, at that time, they were right. The

Vikings were on the island, trapped, and the only way they could get to the English was through the water, across the causeway. Then they'd have to climb the bank, and the English could chop them down one by one. Irene knew that, too, wouldn't be the way it would happen. She wondered how the men around her would feel if they knew what was going to occur.

After listening for some time she learned that she was one of three sons of Odda. She had brothers named Godrinc and Godwig. The three young men were not noted for their bravery. Odda was a rather wealthy and deceased supporter of King Aethelred. For that reason Godric was allowed to join Byrhtnoth's personal troops for the day. Irene watched the men, comparing the quality and costliness of their battle gear and their weapons to those of the villagers, farmers, and tradesmen behind him, whom they were sworn to protect. It wasn't apparent that Byrhtnoth's retinue ever gave a single thought to the condition or safety of the serfs in battle.

One of the well-armored young men was hawking while waiting for the battle to start. It might have been a show of bravery, to indicate how unconcerned he was. Others still sat on their horses, waiting, talking, listening to the Vikings across the river shouting insults. Then, all at once, things began to happen.

Byrhtnoth appeared, on his great white horse. He glistened in his polished battle armor. His white hair spilled out under his helmet. His beard—Irene realized that of them all, only he had a beard—was long and split in the middle, forked. His eyes glared from man to man. Then he passed on to survey the situation near the ford.

"God save him," murmured Aelfwine.

"He doesn't look as if he'd need God's help," said Irene, awed by Byrhtnoth's appearance.

"We all will," said Wulfstan.

"What do you mean?" asked Aelfwine. "Do you think those weasels over there are going to give us any trouble?"

Wulfstan laughed loudly. "No, no!" he said. "I was meaning only that no one can hope to succeed against the Lord's will. We must not take the name of the Lord in vain."

Aelfwine looked embarrassed. "You are right," he said, subdued.

"Your namesake, Godric," said Wulfmaer. Irene looked up

to see the man that Wulfmaer meant, and immediately recalled that there had been two men named Godric in the poem. That was important, but again she couldn't remember why. She cursed Glorian and his trick of disappearing at all the most inconvenient times. Godric, Godric, Godric. Helplessly, Irene waited.

The giant Wulfstan must have noticed Irene's expression and misinterpreted it. "No need for fear, Godric," he said. "It's an easy day, today. Just hacking and hewing." Again he laughed loudly. "Hacking and hewing," he said.

There would be that, all right, but Irene knew that it wouldn't be in the way Wulfstan foresaw.

A tension had been spreading among the men, from the back of the army, among the men who couldn't see and didn't know what was going on, toward the front. "Not long, now," said Aelfwine.

"No, I guess not," said Irene. She felt her bowels loosening, and she wanted to vomit, and she wanted to faint on the grass, and her body was beginning to shift into full, all-out panic.

Wulfstan brought an oaken shield and gave it to her. Wulfstan was again scornful. "It's like a son of Odda to forget his shield, too. There is a man behind you who will not have use of it. Don't forget him, because now *you* will be his shield."

Irene was glad to have the shield, but the contempt in Wulfstan's voice stung. Godric was not well loved in Essex.

Irene had a knife on a pole, and a shield. With this she was expected to stand in front of the massed fury of a Viking raiding party that had been sacking cities up and down the coast. The shield was not much protection, and it actually hampered her. The scramasax was not the most terrible of weapons, either.

Wulfstan, evidently a captain of the household force, was arranging his men. Irene found herself stationed between Eadmaer and a scarred veteran named Toragend. Now the main occupation of the warriors was getting themselves worked up by yelling obscene taunts to the Vikings. Irene was surprised by the profound depth the Anglo-Saxons showed in their repertoire of obscenity. A lot of it had remained in the English language virtually unchanged into Irene's century. Other words and usages were foreign to her. Imagining the meanings of these new foul sayings would be the most enjoyable part of the afternoon.

Byrhtnoth rode by again and stopped in front of his household force. He held up his shield for silence, and there was immediate silence. Byrhtnoth waited a moment, then lowered his shield. He spoke loudly, in a clear and firm voice. To Irene, he did not seem like a man of sixty-five. But then, of course, she did not seem to herself like a woman of eighty-two.

"Listen," cried Byrhtnoth. "Men of Essex, those of you on horses, dismount, and then drive your horses away. That way no one will be tempted to leave early. I will punish a coward more harshly than I will these Vikings." The men who were still on horseback jumped down and sent their horses off toward the forest behind them. "You, son of Offa, this is not the time to play at hawking." The young man was chagrined, but let his bird fly off. The young man took his place in the battle line. The earl rode up and down, giving orders to his men, checking their formation, their weapons, encouraging some, joking with others, until he was satisfied. Then he, too, dismounted and sent his beautiful horse away.

A messenger from the Vikings appeared at the opposite end of the ford. He shouted across a contemptuous offer. If the English would pay a tribute in gold, the Vikings would not slaughter them, but they would leave them in peace. Irene wondered how much they wanted, and if someone could take up a collection. The huge Wulfstan moved forward to answer this sneering Viking, but before he could say a word, Byrhtnoth himself spoke. He did not shout, but his loud voice carried well across the water. "Listen," he said, "all the tribute you'll get from us today will be spears and swords, that's it. Come and get them if you want, but take the message back. We're defending this land, for Aethelred and his people. I have a feeling that there will be a lot of dead Vikings piled around here." He motioned for the front ranks of soldiers to come up right to the river-bank. There was more shouting of threats and challenges, but the distance was too great for anything more. "Wulfstan," said Byrhtnoth, "this battleground belongs to you, doesn't it?"

"It's my land, sir, all right," said the giant.

"Then you go stand at the end of the causeway."

Wulfstan smiled and did as he was ordered. He shook his ash spear and his shield at the Vikings. Two more men went with him and they guarded the way. One of the Vikings, goaded by his fellows, charged through the shallow water over the bridge. He swung an ax at Wulfstan, who caught the blow on his shield. The strength of the blow dropped Wulfstan to one knee, but he stabbed upward at the same time with his spear. The Viking's ax was stuck in the shield, and Wulfstan killed the first of the invaders. He turned, wresting out the ax, and threw it up on the bank.

"All right," shouted one of the men, "that's it!"

"Good work, Wulfstan!"

Wulfstan laughed and turned back to face the Vikings.

One of the Vikings, evidently the leader, called across the water to Byrhtnoth. "Hey," he shouted, "we can't get across this water. You can see that. It's not a fair fight. We can only come across one or two at a time. Let us cross to your side in safety, and we will draw up our army, and you can draw up yours, and we'll have a good battle. Then we'll see whose bodies will be piled around."

"Don't do it," thought Irene, concentrating as hard as she could.

"All right," called Byrhtnoth.

The Vikings began crossing the ford, shouting and laughing. Byrhtnoth ordered his men to lock their shields to make a wall. The men behind were ordered to hold their shields over their heads, defending both themselves and the men in the front rank. "This is it," cried the earl. "This is our land. This is the last time these rats will bother us about anything." Then he turned back to the fight.

Irene was terrified. She almost dropped her weapon. She knew that he had spoken the truth, that this was the last time the Vikings would trouble this particular band of men. "Glorian!" she called.

"What's that?" asked Eadmaer. "A prayer for glory?"

"Urn," said Irene.

"You'll have your chance today."

"Urn."

Then it started. Men began shouting all around Irene. The noise on the battlefield from the two armies was almost deafening, and they hadn't even begun the actual fighting. Irene thought that the yelling would stop when the fighting started.

The Vikings rushed. The din of ax biting shield, of men crying out the end of their lives, the clash of metal against metal filled the air. Men fell on both sides, slashed and hacked so badly that tears filled Irene's eyes. For a moment she couldn't see clearly. In her worst imaginings, she had never pictured anything as terrible as this. She blinked several times, and saw that Wulfmaer, Byrhtnoth's own nephew, was wounded badly. The young man died not far from her. He was avenged immediately, but the Englishman who struck out so boldly was himself cut down.

"We'll get them, now!" cried Toragend.

"I want my first one," said Eadmaer.

"Stand firm," said Wulfstan. "Byrhtnoth's watching us. Stand firm. Keep the shield wall."

Irene was glad to keep the shield wall. She put her mind to keeping her shield in place with those on either side. She tried to take her mind off the sounds of men, many men, dying so close to her, and the fact that she herself would soon—

No, she would not think it. Glorian would not have led her into something like that.

She saw Byrhtnoth himself go forward to meet a Viking churl. The Viking wounded the earl with a spear. Byrhtnoth, rising up to his full height, glared down at the Viking. With the edge of his shield he split the spear, and the haft sprang away. The point was still in him, and he was wounded, but he seemed not to mind. Irene watched, captured by the strength and irresistible force of the man.

Byrhtnoth was enraged. He struck with his own spear, first piercing the Viking's throat, then again, strongly, breaking the man's chain mail, and stabbing into the Viking's heart. The earl looked skyward and laughed. There were cheers around him.

And then he was wounded again. A spear thrown by one of the Vikings struck him. A young man—Irene could see that it was Aelfwine—pulled the spear from Byrhtnoth's body and threw it back, killing one of the enemy.

The Vikings were all vying for the chance to finish off Byrhtnoth, because he was wearing a small fortune in gold and jewelry. His sword as well had a golden hilt and guard. The earl drew the sword, but a Viking's ax dismembered him. Byrhtnoth still would not fall. His sword at his feet, his strong arm cut off, wounded by spear points, still he shouted defiance until the Vikings closed in on him. Irene could hear the deep voice of Byrhtnoth praying, thanking the Lord for all the worldly joys he had known, and asking that his soul be taken into heaven. A moment later he was dead. His part was over in this battle of no significance.

The two men who stood beside the earl, stunned somewhat, gave up their lives trying to defend him. The Vikings were beginning to break apart the English formation. Irene dropped her long-handled knife first, and then her shield. She heard cries of anger and dismay from the soldiers around her, but all she could see was the body of Byrthnoth, the most noble man she had ever met, lying hacked to pieces on the ground, almost at her feet. And as she watched, more good men fell.

Irene turned. Her strong young man's body pushed her through the ranks. Men behind were beginning to cry out in confusion. She saw far ahead of her the quiet forest, two miles away, but nearer were the horses. She broke free of the struggle and ran to the beautiful horse of Byrhtnoth. She caught the beast and mounted it, then rode for the forest. She heard shouts behind her, men thinking that the earl himself had abandoned them, men in the rear who did not know that their leader was already dead. More men began to flee. Irene was only barely conscious. Her mind was numb. She was aware that two other men were following her on horseback. "Godrinc and Godwig," she thought. "My brothers."

And then she knew who the two Godrics were, one cowardly and one bound by the Saxon-Germanic ideal of total loyalty to one's leader. Irene knew which Godric she had been.

Chapter Eight

Clean. Really Clean

Galloping at full speed through a forest is inadvisable. This was a fact that Irene learned through experience. She had been learning quite a bit lately through experience and, though it was tougher, she appreciated every bit of new knowledge. Now she knew that galloping through a forest made the low-hanging branches jump at her much faster.

When she slowed the great horse down, she caught her own breath. She began to relax a little, but not completely. The memory of what she had seen, what was happening at Maldon when she fled, and—what she knew from the booklet—what was going to occur made her uneasy. Guilt surged through her and almost made her break down completely. She had learned by heart some of the speeches of Byrhtnoth's most loyal *heorthwerod* lieutenants, ones they had spoken as they fought on hopelessly, finally, while they were dying. One of the eldest of these men, at the very end, called on the few remaining Anglo-Saxon English with words that would keep their emotional significance forever: "Our will shall be the harder, heart the fiercer, courage the greater, as our strength lessens."

Escaping on Byrhtnoth's beautiful white horse, Irene felt almost like goading the beast to full gallop again and meeting one of those low-hanging branches as soon as Fate decided. But she did not. She had not fled the battlefield to throw her life away so easily. She walked the horse among the trees, searching for a path that led anywhere.

As dusk drew on, Irene was startled to see a small wooden sign on a post. She stopped the horse beside it and read the words.

FIVE SIGNS FROM NOW

Irene had no idea what that meant, but she suspected that there would be another sign soon. Not twenty yards farther, there was.

THERE'LL BE A SIGN

Irene saw that there was a series. She walked by them on the horse, reading each.

AND IF YOU'RE SMART,

YOU'LL READ EACH LINE

GLORIAN

Glorian. Irene shook her head. She could hardly wait to see what the next sign said. She really never wanted to see Glorian again, she never wanted to hear from him, she never wanted—

IRENE!
THE POWERS THAT BE
PROUDLY PRESENT

THE TRAGEDY OF GODRIC OF ESSEX

Featuring IRENE
With HONEST RUSTIC
Directed by GLORIAN
Produced by THE POWERS THAT BE

Irene stared at the sign for a long time. It made her feel very peculiar. She felt as though she weren't really there, as if she had been drugged, or if she were dreaming or delirious. Perhaps, she thought, she had been injured in battle and she *was* delirious. She didn't hurt anywhere, though, except at the points where her body made contact with Byrthnoth's horse and saddle, and she understood that well enough.

She wiped her brow. She was perspiring heavily. She was breathing hard. It was getting too dark to ride, so she dismounted and led the horse. Then after a while she turned the horse around and swatted it, and it trotted away back toward the battlefield. Irene felt it belonged near its noble, fallen master.

She was so tired that she had to sit. A great tree was down across her path, and she climbed up and sat on it. She wiped her brow again and felt how fast her heart was beating. "Now falls due the bitter note of cowardice," she thought. A breeze blew, and she was thankful; she felt a lot better. She gazed up at the sky, where a few stars were already visible. "For as I rode," she thought, "the chillest airs of flight—"

What was this nonsense? She started over again. She said aloud,

Now falls due the bitter note of cowardice,
For, as I rode, the chillest airs of flight
Had iced these thoughts of shame and still'd my mind.

Irene's eyes opened wider. Her teeth clenched in anger. Iambic pentameter. Imitation Elizabethan meter and language. *The Tragedy of Godric of Essex,*

Directed by GLORIAN. Probably written by him, too. "I'll strangle him," she thought. She tried to say the words, but they wouldn't come out. She tried to sit still and say nothing, but she learned she couldn't do that, either. She had to take it from the top and go through the scene.

IRENE: Now falls due the bitter note of cowardice,
      For, as I rode, the chillest airs of flight
      Had iced these thoughts of shame and still'd my mind.
      Now to what eerie land have I been drawn
      That, thus exiled, with pain for company,
      Those dark lords, Fear and Dread, may spring conceal'd
      And force like simple brigands what of peace
      Remains to me?

(Enter a Rustic)

RUSTIC: Good my lord, I bid you pleasant time of day.

IRENE: And so to you, my honest man. What realm
      Is this, where chance and misfortune have led?
      Whose limits have I, all in innocence,
      Defied, wand'ring ignorant and in want?
      Whose law binds you, whose power claims your love?

RUSTIC: Know you not, my lord? Then, marry, were it best
      To wander hence and seek your rest away
      In more auspicious lands. Here rules no King
      but our many-troubled selves.

IRENE: However badly starred you mayest be,
      Still would I match you grief for cruelest grief.
      Though stranger to me is your nation's name,
      What suff'ring it endures, what foul intrigues,
      What unimagined woes that woke to life
      But as the babe its mother's breast first sought,
      These ills, as yours, will ne'er with mine compare.

"How do I get out of this?" she wondered. She looked around for Glorian but he was, of course, nowhere in sight. He was probably waiting in the wings, or sitting in the front or last row, or waiting across the street from the forest in a bar, to hear the reactions of the members of the audience as they came out. "How do I get out of this? I'll concentrate on keeping my mouth shut."

RUSTIC: Good lord, you seem to me the Ithacan,
      The cursed of the gods, that clever King,
      Odysseus; upon a foreign land
      Without his princely name, or gold, or friend,
      The fickle poison sea had flung him up.
      Look you but the fame he heap'd upon himself.
      By means of crafty guile and honey'd speech
      He won these favors: those of goddesses
      And mortal scepter'd hands in unknown states,
      Who neither glanced the webbings of his tongue.
      Such riches that he won he won alone.
      You may find much to emulate, and what

Of cleverness that stings too like evil
You may despise. Being alone, this test
May mark your virtue on your brow.

"I won't," thought Irene. She refused to speak. Knowing Glorian, if this insane encounter went on much longer he might book her into the forest circuit for the rest of the season. She tried to hold back. The rustic fidgeted. He repeated the cue.

RUSTIC: May mark your virtue on your brow.

Irene was helpless. She hated being helpless, and she hated it even worse when it was Glorian's fault.

IRENE: I wonder at this nation's governing!
      What pleasant sleep the counselors must enjoy,
      For now I see the proper burial
      of ancient strife and common argument.
      What troubles do you claim, where peasants speak
      With ornaments of ermin'd noblemen?
      A general of this conceit must know
      The hardship that is government; no cries
      For gold from lowly throats to frugal crown I
      No enmity toward those of birth and blood!
      A daisy chain of stations up to God,
      With hand upheld to willing helping hand.
      Here even—man is known as what he is,
      Divisive futile factions die stillborn,
      And pride of place is fluent through the land.
      What happy men! Yes, such dangers that offend
      Yourselves must need derive from bordered, grim,
      And envious lands. I pledge my bladed arm
      Defensive to yourself and countrymen,
      Philosophers unstained by war's wisdom.
      For though the low make pleasant-scented speech,
      With nods to Homer as embellishment,
      The mounted armors of the enemy
      May fail to stay their swords for fair discourse.

RUSTIC: Good sir, you do not apprehend the source
              And tide of our regret.

"Glorian!" thought Irene. "Glorian, stop it!"

"Once more," came Glorian's voice in her mind. "Once more, Irene, and give it some *feeling*."

"I'll kill you, Glorian."

"You can't, Irene. Come on. One more line."

"I'll find a way."

IRENE: Tis as well. My temper lacks such senselessness
              As benefits the bloody valiant.

"Got you!" cried Glorian, stepping out from behind a nearby tree.

"You—"

"Wait a minute, Irene." Glorian turned to the rustic. "There's a great horse walking that way, and if you run you can have it. You'll see that it's the horse of a nobleman, and the bridle and saddle alone are worth a duke's ransom."

"My lords," said the man hurriedly, "thank you!" He ran after Byrhtnoth's horse.

"What is he going to do with that horse? They'll hang him for stealing it," said Irene.

"Don't worry," said Glorian mildly. "Neither he nor the horse exist anymore."

"Ah," said Irene, feeling fury rise in her, "and do you? Do I? And the army, and the Vikings, and the butchering, and—"

"Calm down, calm down," said Glorian. He was now of average height, slim rather than muscular, with dark skin. He had black, curly hair. He was wearing a loose tunic of yellow-green, with ruffled sleeves, over green hose. He wore a large jasper ring on each hand. "This is what is known as debriefing," he said.

"Is that what it is?" cried Irene. She looked around for something to hit him with.

"Here," he said. He held her scramasax, the one she had dropped as she had fled the battlefield.

"No!" she screamed, then broke down into tears. He held her for a few moments.

"There, there," he said softly. "There, there."

"Nothing," she said, "nothing, nothing in the world could be worth what you've put me through."

"I wasn't sure, myself," he said. "I was confused. Normally the situation is a bit different. But it was the glass, your precious Depression glass. It changed everything. Running was the only reasonable thing for you to do. I was held back. I've never been prevented from helping out, until this time. Something big is going on, Irene, and whatever it is it centers on you, and it's too late to slip off. You've got to tough it out from here on."

Irene got control of herself. She sniffed a couple of times and then spoke. "I can't," she said.

"You can. The last lines you spoke, 'My temper lacks such senselessness as benefits the bloody valiant.' That did it. That saved you. Don't worry. I'll be with you most of the way."

"Most? Most?"

"I'm leaving you now. *I* have to be prepared, believe it or not. I haven't been recalled, my goodness, I don't remember the last time. In the meanwhile, you're going to have to make a small arbitrary payment for the lives you cost at Maldon."

Irene slapped Glorian. He stared, then raised a hand slowly. Irene saw that the mark of her hand was still on his cheek. "It's true," he said. "Anyone else, the episode at Maldon would have been fine. On to the next trial. But you can't make it through 'good.' You have to be perfect."

"What's going to—"

Glorian was gone.

Irene was alone in the forest. It was dark, and she was very hungry. Through the trees she could see the flickering light of a fire. She walked that way as quietly and cautiously as she could. She saw a campsite. There were black-iron frying pans on the fire, bacon and eggs frying, stew bubbling in a pot, coffee, and a loaf of bread wrapped in cellophane. There were no packs, sleeping rolls, or other indications that the campsite belonged to anyone else. Irene decided that Glorian had left it for her. She helped herself to the food, took care of the fire, and then stretched out to sleep.

The next morning she woke up and it was freezing cold. There was about 2 ½ feet of snow on the ground, and drifts so high that they almost covered the garages of the houses along East 147th Street. Irene was cold. She shivered as she tried in vain to relight the cooking fire. She would have to do without breakfast. The fire, she realized as she became more aware of her surroundings, was in the middle of a narrow red-brick street. Two-family houses lined the street, and between the street and the sidewalks were tree lawns of barren sycamores. A wind came up and blew snow over every sign of the campsite, and there was no more forest. Irene was somewhere.

Not far from her, lying on the snow, was a heavy, zippered coat. She put it on, grateful for the protection it gave her from the cold. She found gloves in one pocket, and put them on. She found earmuffs in the other pocket, wondered what they were for a short while, then untwisted them and put them on. A little farther were a pair of rubber galoshes with buckles. She put them on, too. She was cold, but she was not suffering the way she would if these things had not been provided. She started walking along East 147th Street. Soon she came to a small cross street. She wondered if she should go straight, or turn left at Lytton. She looked down the smaller street and saw, not far from her feet, a long wooden dowel with a yellow canvas flag at the end. That was her sign, and she picked the flag up and walked along Lytton. Two blocks later, at East 149th Street, there was a school for young children.

"That way," said one of the small girls, pointing to the left. Irene nodded and went that way. When she got to the corner there was another young man, a bit older than Irene's male body, similarly dressed now, also holding a yellow flag on a stick. "Say," said the man.

Irene noticed that the man was odd-looking. His skin was frightening. At Maldon, many of the Anglo-Saxons had made strange designs in their skin by puncturing dozens of holes and forcing some material permanently beneath. But this young man was dark brown, almost black all over, as if he had been painted. "Who are you?" she asked.

"Name's Bobby O. Brown," he said. Two very young children came up behind them, and he held them back with his flag. He looked down the cross street, which was called Lucknow, and there was no traffic. He checked for turning cars from 149th, and then opened his flag to let the children cross the street.

"Bobby O. Brown," Irene said, "you have a funny look."

Two men came up behind her. One was dressed in a dark robe, with a hood over his head. He seemed timid. The other, tall and proud, was dressed in a white toga and wore a wreath of laurel. Irene did as Brown had done, and then let the two men cross. "Dante and Virgil," said Brown. "Don't worry about them. You haven't seen one of me before?" He didn't seem surprised. He acted as though he had met others who hadn't seen one before.

"No, I'm sorry, and I hope you don't take offense."

"No offense," said Bobby O. Brown. "I'm a black."

"I can see that," said Irene. "Does it give you pain?"

"It used to," he said. "Sometimes, you see, people called us blacks. That was the time I was from. Because we're black, just the way you're white. Sometimes they called us Negroes, which comes from the Spanish *negro*, from the Latin *niger*. Sometimes they called us colored people. Sometimes, oh, sometimes they called us all sorts of things from darkies to—"

"Look out!" cried Irene. One little girl, perhaps five years old, had ignored their flags and was crossing Lucknow. A car, a 1957 Chevrolet, blue and white, hardtop, was coming toward her, driving a little too recklessly for the street conditions. The driver jammed on the brakes, but the car kept coming. Irene dropped her flag and leaped. She threw the girl out of the car's path, and the Chevrolet stopped not more than two inches from Irene's own body. She lay prostrate in the snow, her heart beating fast and loud. The snow was getting in the sleeves of her jacket and down her neck, and the feeling was intensely unpleasant. It was very cold. She raised herself on hands and knees, took her flag again, and stood. She felt light-headed.

"That's one," said Bobby O. Brown.

The little girl was nowhere in sight. Neither was the car.

"I don't understand," she said, panting.

"Next one's mine," said the man.

"Fine," said Irene, "entirely fine by me. What is it?"

"We're working off things. I'm working off, well, I know what

I'm working off. And you're working off something, no doubt, nothing that will kill you forever, something just bad enough to put you on this corner for a while until you're all good again."

"I caused the deaths of some people, I think. I exhibited cowardice."

"Oh," said Bobby O. Brown.

Another group of children approached, from the other side of Lucknow. Irene checked all around, and there was no traffic at all. She stepped into the street, in the snow, and held out her flag protectively. The little children began crossing.

A car squealed around a corner and straight at all of them.

"Look out," said Bobby O. Brown, rather calmly. He jumped, knocking Irene and the children out of the path of the car. The car, a Ford Fairlane in bad need of body work, stopped very, very close to his head and chest. He took his time getting up.

"Uh," said Irene, still shaking the snow from her jacket and trying to dry her hands off before putting the gloves back on, "how often does this happen?"

"All the time," said Brown. "*All* the time. They aren't here, you see, but we are. They're here for us. That's why we're here."

"Oh, oh," said Irene, getting the idea at last. "We're showing that we have wonderful qualities of courage and devotion. Ha, ha. How dumb."

"Yeah. It's cold."

"Cold," said Irene, stamping her feet and slapping her hands together.

"They keep it at four below. Fahrenheit. I don't know what that would be Celsius."

"Negro, eh?" said Irene.

"I suppose." There was a long, uncomfortable silence.

"Well, do you prefer darkie, or—"

She leaped forward to save the lives of a few children. She was getting a little nonchalant about it. "We don't get hurt, do we?"

"We're not supposed to," said Brown. "And call me a black, if you have to call me anything, which you won't, unless you strike up a conversation with one of these kids."

"Fine," she said. "What are you in for?"

"Point-shaving," he said.

"Making spears?"

"No," he said, laughing. "I used to play basketball. I used to take money from these guys and I would miss baskets. I was the star, I mean, the whole *franchise* of this team, and if I didn't get my points, the team lost. So some nights I was paid off not to get my points."

"I suppose that's awful," said Irene. She saw another three children coming toward her. This group would be Brown's turn.

"I don't know," he said, looking at her with a strange expression, "there are worse things."

"Look out!" she yelled. Brown turned, almost mechanically, and without any evident emotion saved the lives of the children. Irene wondered how long she'd have to spend at the corner of Lucknow and East 149th.

Hours went by, days, weeks, there was no way of counting time, because the sun didn't move and there were no flows of activity that might have signaled the beginnings or ends of days. Just the frequent arrival of children, some crossing the street in one direction, some going the other way. Irene and Brown took turns saving lives with uncommon heroism. It was unbearably tedious.

"You know," she said, "I've never seen one of these automobiles before, and I've never seen houses or streets like these, and I've never seen a black before, and it must be years since Alyse was this young, and before that it was thirty years or since I've seen children. But somehow I feel like I belong."

"That's what purgatory's all about," said Brown, yawning.

"That's what this is? Purgatory?"

"Well," he said, "really, it's Cleveland."

"Cleveland," said Irene wonderingly. She had heard ancient tales about a long-dead city named Cleveland. She told Brown.

"You're from a different time than I am," he said. "When I was doing my thing, shaving points, Cleveland was a big city. But even then people would have testified that it was long dead."

"I don't understand," said Irene.

"You don't have to," said Brown, watching Irene jump to save a bundled-up little boy with blond hair and a cute girl with long black hair. "You won't be here long."

"Why not?"

"You've almost worked off your offense. I can tell. The cars are stopping farther and farther from you."

Irene felt glad. "How about you?" she asked.

Brown looked down at the filthy snow. He kicked a lump of it. "I'm here for a long time," he said. "I've seen a lot of people come and go on this corner."

"Why should you be punished more than I?"

"I made a bad mistake."

Irene was bewildered. "I cost lives. I made soldiers desert, leading to other lives lost. An entire army was slaughtered, and I had a major role in the disaster. All that you did was throw a couple of meaningless sporting events."

Brown looked at her thoughtfully for a moment. He leaped out and pushed twin red-haired girls, nearly spherical in shape in their snowsuits, to safety. His handsome black face and beard came up freckled with snow. He swiped it away. "I threw some basketball games. I made the mistake of throwing one when the good guys were cheering for us. The crime wasn't so severe. It was getting caught. And back then, man, I didn't even believe in the good guys and the bad guys."

"Do you know Glorian?" asked Irene.

Brown looked stunned, "Glorian?" he said in a soft voice. "He took me from Foster Park in Brooklyn and got me into Providence, and then two years I played for the Bullets, and then—"

"You got caught."

"I didn't think he'd notice."

Irene saved the lives of three children, who cried and shouted at her for pushing them down. The car was gone before she stood up. There were tire tracks in the snow, however, and in one of the tire tracks was a piece of glass. A light blue piece of Depression glass, blue like sky, madonna blue. Irene recognized it as a Mayfair partitioned celery dish. She picked it up carefully, wiping the snow and sludge from it, and put it in her bag.

"You're going soon," said Brown.

"I suppose," said Irene. "Does that mean I've paid for my cowardice?"

"Yes."

"The whole thing is stupid."

"Yes."

"I'll put in a good word for you," she said. She watched him save a few lives.

"Don't bother," said Brown, standing up. "Dozens have. The Powers That Be don't easily forgive you when you jazz them. People they can spare. Battles, war. Whatever they lose to the other side on sports events, things like that, wheat futures, television program ratings, those they don't forget."

"They bet on your basketball game?"

"That's the way it was explained to me. The bad guys have a good thing going for themselves. Far away, all the way across the country, and the Powers That Be war against them. One of the ways, I guess, is by staging their struggles through us. That one basketball game was one chapter in the eternal fight for good against evil, and I shaved points from the wrong side. I'll be here a long time."

"Can I light a candle for you? A prayer?"

"Glorian, you say. You know Glorian. Use him. Leverage. Bargain. I'd like to get out of here. It's cold."

"Yes," said Irene. She saved the lives of two children who would have met death beneath the skidding wheels of a Nash Rambler. "It's cold."

"Yeah," said Bobby O. Brown, "and I hate kids."

Glorian appeared suddenly, in a burst of light so brilliant that both Irene and Brown had to shield their eyes. "Irene," he said.

"Look," she said angrily, "I hate the way you're treating me. Like some puppet following your foolish directions, and you don't even offer me the courtesy to tell me what to expect and what to do."

"We have to observe your natural behavior," he said calmly, ignoring Brown altogether.

"Forget it," she said. "Brown, this black man here, has been treated very badly, and so have I. I demand apologies."

"You are in no position to demand anything," said Glorian. Despite the minus-four-degree temperature, he was wearing his Cub Scout uniform. Brown was trying to decide whether to let them argue, or help him across the street. Glorian looked like he was ten years old.

"Glorian!" cried Irene. "You have no respect for me at all. I'm just a marker in your game. I refuse to go on. I'll stand on this corner forever if I have to, saving little children over and over again through eternity, before I allow myself to be used."

"Don't say it," said Brown. "I've been here a while, and it gets very boring. And cold."

"You haven't even noticed," said Glorian, sounding a little hurt. "I've made Webelos. See the insignia on the cap? The different neckerchief? The Arrow of Light. The Webelos badge?"

Irene refused to say a word. A car bore down on a group of four children. Brown was about to jump for them, but Irene stopped him. The car swerved around the corner, missing the children by the smallest margin allowable in purgatory. The children screamed with delight.

"That," said Glorian in a cold, harsh voice, "may have sealed your fate. There are worse places, you know."

"There were others here before you," she said, almost joyfully. She took out the Mayfair celery dish and showed it to him.

Glorian's expression, fleetingly, almost imperceptibly, was fearful. He said nothing for a moment. He looked as though the essential significance of the universe had just been nullified. "They?" he said. "Here?"

Irene packed the celery dish away again. She indicated Brown. "Glorian," she said, "get us out of here."

There was another brilliant flash of light. Irene was back in the forest, and Glorian was beside her, carrying two bags, dressed in the light yellow-green tunic and green hose that he had worn earlier. "Where's Bobby O. Brown?" she asked.

"Ah," said Glorian, smiling, "he just came off the bench in the last seconds of play. He blocked a shot, caught the rebound off the glass, dribbled it downcourt, and stuffed it in at the buzzer for the win."

"And the children?" asked Irene. "At the corner of Lucknow and 149th Street?"

"Survival of the fittest," said Glorian. He shrugged.

Chapter Nine

The Second, Third, Maybe Fourth Surprises of a Lifetime (A Long Chapter)

Glorian marched through the thinning woods as though he alone had a purpose, and Irene followed behind him because she knew that, in fact, he *did* have a purpose, and she had a purpose—which was getting to California—and he was helping her, and if he chose to be afraid or sulk or whatever, he could. She would not expect perfect behavior from Glorian, even though apparently he belonged to a group of Powers that expected exactly that from their proteges.

Glorian did not even turn around until they came to a small creek. Ahead of them Irene could see through the trees to a clearing. There were no more trees beyond, as if all the forest in the world would come to an end soon, forever. She did not know what that meant. She had never in her life been out of the forest except for artificial situations, such as Maldon and purgatory. These things were fantasy. The forest was the world. But in the direction the creek was flowing, it appeared that there was nothing but open space.

"Irene," said Glorian. He had stopped beside the creek and was staring ahead, where she was looking.

"Yes, Glorian?"

"Do you still have that last piece of Depression glass that you found in the snow of purgatory?"

"Yes," she said. "I have it packed in my bag."

"Would you mind, would you be offended in any way, if I were to ask you to open your bag, take out that piece of glass, and put it on the ground? Would you understand?"

"No," she said.

"I will explain." There was a moment of silence. "Well, really, I can't explain why, now, but that particular piece of glass represents a danger to me. This has been used to stall—not defeat—me in one or two previous incidents. It is a tactic of the enemy that is petty, bothersome, ineffective in the long run, and merely annoying. Still, I would feel safer if that madonna blue Mayfair partitioned celery dish were in my bags rather than yours. I don't want you to think that I don't trust you, but there is the chance that one of the enemy might seek to lead you astray in some manner."

"Sure, sure," said Irene. "I don't care. Here." She opened her backpack and took out the glass. She put it on the ground between them.

"Thank you, Irene," said Glorian. "Take this vial of powder and sprinkle it over the celery dish." She did so. "Take these two candles, place them beside the celery dish, and light them with these matches." She did so. "Light these sticks of incense and put them in the ground around the celery dish." She did so. "Now, move away." She did so, curious. Glorian stood over the celery dish and muttered a long charm. "Turn away," he warned. Once more, she did as she was instructed. There was a blinding flash of light. When Irene looked back, the celery dish had been transformed into a handled sandwich server. "You may have this," he said.

"Thank you. It isn't a threat?"

"Don't be silly," said Glorian. "Who has ever been threatened by a sandwich server? Pack it away."

It was a handsome addition to her collection, and she packed it carefully. She saw that Glorian was already walking away, toward the end of the forest.

"Don't I get an explanation of the battle," she asked, "and the way I acted, and where you went, and purgatory, and why I was there if I acted the way I was supposed to, and why we're here now?"

Glorian turned and looked at her. He almost glared. "You were not a transcendent sacrifice, after all," he said, evidently disappointed. "If anything, you were *subs*cendent."

"That's hardly fair," she said, annoyed. "You skipped out at the first chance."

"I have my ways," he said in simple explanation.

"Sometimes they're lousy ways," she said.

"That does it," said Glorian. He turned and started to walk back into the forest.

"Where are you going?" asked Irene.

"I'm giving up on you," he said. "I thought it was obvious. There's not a chance in the world that you will serve the Powers That Be, that you will go on to achieve your potential, that—"

He was interrupted by a blinding flash of light. A handsome young man, naked except for a vague cloud below his lower abdomen, with wings on his feet, appeared. "She is saved," said the young man.

"Thank you," said Irene. "Can I have my old body back?"

"She is *not* saved, and I say so," said Glorian.

"She is saved, I have the message direct," said Hermes.

"Well, then," said Glorian huffily, "well, if I'm going to be overruled at every turn, then what's the use of my going on, anyway? Why don't *you* just take her on? Why doesn't the great Hermes lead this old lady to California? Or do you have more important things to do?"

"I have more important things to do," said Hermes. "I have messages to deliver. This was one of them. Farewell." There was another blinding flash.

"That was Hermes?" asked Irene.

"Hate his guts," said Glorian. "I really do. Let's go, then, as long as you're saved." He turned again and headed out of the forest. "Come on, if you're coming."

"Glorian?"

"Come on. The forest ends in twenty-five yards. Then there is the Mississippi River. It is something few people have ever seen. It will be something to tell your grandniece about."

"That is the Mississippi River there?" she asked.

"Yes," he said, smiling, "right. Everything's running smoothly again. Let's get on with it."

"You know what, Glorian?" said Irene. "I think you could use a century or so in purgatory, falling on your face in the snow to save someone else."

"Irene, you're hostile. You're making me seem like an arbitrary, villainous, and hateful person. No. I have my instructions, and I can assure you that I'm following them to the letter. The instructions are from—"

"I know."

"Anyway, they're more important than anything you want to do or anything I want to do. And my instructions were to get you into the Battle of Maldon and to leave you. To rescue you from purgatory—"

"*Rescue* me?"

"How else did you think you got out?"

"Never mind."

Glorian breathed heavily. "And," he said, "my instructions were to change you back into an old person after we crossed the bridge over the river."

"I'm sorry, Glorian," she said. "I'm really kind of sorry."

"I am, too, Irene, because I really love you. But you're not just a cog in a cosmic wheel, my friend. I've led many others, and they were just cogs in the cosmic wheel. Irene, you're a whole new cosmic wheel all to yourself, and you've got to go through the stages. You're like a butterfly."

She shook her head, not comprehending what Glorian was telling her. "You love me, Glorian?"

"I have come to."

"I don't know how I feel about you," she said.

"That is not important." They had walked up to one end of a long, straight bridge, made of steel, painted pale blue, unmarked by stains, or wind, or weather, or age. "This bridge was built many years ago, so long a time that it is measured in centuries. There used to be a civilization in this land, and that culture is the one that operated the 'cities' you hear so much about. It is impossible to describe the wonders of their world. Things that flew in the sky, that sailed beneath the sea, that talked around the world in seconds, things that your dreams and nightmares only sketch. But as their world ended, as it had to, the people came together to decide what they would do."

"Why did their world have to end?" she asked.

"Because they were eating the world to make it into what they wanted, and their hunger was growing faster than their achievements. So, in the last days, on this continent, at least—"

"There are others, then," said Irene.

"Yes. Where was I? Oh, well, from the Mississippi River, which you see below us, all the way to the Atlantic Ocean, the cities disappeared without a trace. Forests reclaimed the land, and that is what we have today. There is unbroken forest for hundreds and hundreds of miles, stretching from this point east, past the house of Michael and Constance, to the vast blue Atlantic. West of us"—Glorian pointed across the bridge—"there used to be a land of plain and prairie, also dotted with great cities. The old people, deciding on a mark that would memorialize them for all time to come, decided to eradicate those cities as well. To the west, there are the Rocky Mountains, a natural barrier. They are very far away. Between the Mississippi River and the Rocky Mountains the old people worked to level the land. Hills and mountains and bulges in the Earth itself disappeared. North to south, east to west, the land between river and mountains was made level, flat, like the surface of the dining table of Michael and Constance. And then finally, as the master stroke, the old people covered this plain with Teflon."

"What is that?" asked Irene.

"It is a synthetic material developed by the DuPont Company centuries ago. It had been refined and perfected. What covers the Great Plains today is Teflon XVII."

"Why did the old people cover this vast area with Teflon?"

Glorian had to think. "Well," he said at last, "so that nothing would stick to it."

Irene put a hand up to shade her eyes. She looked west. "So between here and the Rocky Mountains, a vast distance, there is absolutely nothing?"

"Exactly."

"That's crazy."

"But it makes you remember the old ones, doesn't it? They were correct to that degree. It's an impressive piece of work. All that remains are the great Teflon reservoirs on the northern boundary. The knowledge of making Teflon, or spreading it on surfaces, or protecting it, is lost. The rivers that flowed into the Mississippi were rerouted below ground, through culverts. The natural rain that falls runs into drains set into the Teflon plain. Everything has been considered."

"And we have to walk across it."

"Yes," said Glorian. "It is difficult. It is more difficult than the Battle of Maldon. Of all the trials, the Teflon beats most of them.

There is no change in physical features. There is nothing to look at. There are no conveniences, except for the occasional 'hotspot.' These are little circular areas that serve as cooking surfaces. They are marked by a broken circular line of red. The red circle is about six inches in diameter, and they are totally invisible from a distance of ten feet. So happening on them is a matter of great luck, particularly as there was no system used in placing them. They are scattered across the great Teflon plain, much as buffalo used to be scattered, and Indians, and people."

"It is a strange world," said Irene. She was hesitant to cross the bridge into it.

"We must go," said Glorian. "Or else you can go back to purgatory and get snow up your sleeves again."

"No, thank you. I will cross the bridge with you."

They started across, and their steps echoed on the steel. The river below was a dark, muddy-brown color. There was little noise, other than the quiet lapping of water and the shrieking of some birds overhead. The walk across the Mississippi River bridge took some time. They came to the end finally, and Glorian congratulated Irene. "We have passed another point of importance," he said.

"A sign."

"Yes," he said, "a sign it is. A sign of your innate goodness, quality, and spiritual value."

"No," said Irene, "I mean there's a sign a little farther ahead, on the plain."

At the end of the bridge there was a narrow crack. Immediately on the other side of the crack, the Teflon plain began. It was inhumanly smooth and perfect. It was that way everywhere. It was the most perfect thing the human race had ever made. But Irene was right. There was a large sign, white, edged in black, with black letters, on a metal post stuck into the brown Teflon a few feet away.

DO NOT TRACK MUD ON PRAIRIE

Irene took one step, and her body changed. She had been in the body of a strong young man for so long, she had grown used to it. But in midstride it changed. It became old again. The leg on the ground wobbled, and the stride was shortened. The next step was slow, small and painful. The joints, all of them, everywhere, wherever there could be an infirmity, there was pain and resistance. Skin hung in wrinkled folds under the elbows, under the chin, and when she reached up hesitantly to touch, beneath the eyes. She could not see well or hear well or move well. Her senses of taste and smell had been reduced to the level they had been before she had left the house of Michael and Constance. "Glorian?" she called. Her voice wavered, and she was embarrassed by it.

"What?" said Glorian, not turning around. "You wanted an old body again, didn't you?"

That was needlessly cruel, thought Irene. The old body was a shock. She wondered why Glorian had had to do it. It seemed petty, too. This was another instance of her loss of control. She wanted her life to be in her hands, yet Glorian had forced an old body on her. She would not have denied it; yet she resented not being asked. She was angered by being ignored—*worse* than ignored, her wishes were batted away like annoying gnats.

"Glorian?"

"What? Irene, come on."

"Glorian, why did you have to do this to me? How can I go on in this body?"

Glorian turned and stared at her. "Your old body seemed good enough to you at the beginning of this adventure. What? Has your opinion changed?"

"My old body was good enough. The young body was better."

"Never satisfied," said Glorian. He waved his hand as though scattering a cloud of gnats.

"Wipe your feet," he said.

Irene clenched her jaws. Because of her old body, it would have been a decision too fine for amateurs to judge if she clenched her teeth. She did not have many. She didn't say a word. She scraped her feet—she was wearing brown oxfords, which had originally been purchased at a neighborhood supermarket—once each, looking at Glorian as though she wanted to scrape him instead. "All right?" she asked. The sound of her voice frightened her. It was low and grating. She did not sound well. She thought she just might die while Glorian was doing his mystical things. She shuddered. She didn't want to die in anyone's body but her own.

"Fine," said Glorian, "let's get moving."

"Wipe your feet," she said. She pointed to the sign and saw that her skin was, oh, her arm was almost translucent, yellowed, with brown spots, fingers gnarled in a way they had never been before, gnarled by many years of—

"Glorian, this is an old *man's* body. This is not my old body."

"What difference does that make?"

"Why am I in another strange body? Give me *my* own body, not someone else's. If it's to be old, let it be *my* old."

"You're doing it again," said Glorian. "You're seeing your life as if it were some constant, unfolding ribbon of a thing. No, Irene, you've lost the right to that kind of life. Now your life is a string of segments, and this segment is being played by Irene in the body of an older man. How does it feel?"

"The old man's body?" she asked. "It took me a while even to notice. It's not much different at all, when you get to this age."

Glorian frowned at her and looked down. He was barefoot, and he was embarrassed that his right foot left a little clump of soil and dead leaves on the bridge. He would have tracked mud on the prairie.

They left the bridge, and Irene knew that they had also left behind everything that was familiar in her life. Maldon was more like the house of Michael and Constance. At least there were trees and people. Here there was nothing, *nothing* that looked the tiniest bit like what the world was supposed to look like. There were no places that rose into rolling hills, no places that ran away from her in jagged chasms or sloping valleys. There were no clumps of trees anywhere, as she looked from left to right. There were no wind-shaped rock formations. There were no fields of gently waving grasses, or sand dunes, or even an occasional lonely cactus. No palm trees. No spreading live oaks. No little thrown-together shacks of poor folk who scratched a poor living from the stingy ground.

There were no physical features other than the Teflon plain. None. Not one.

No physical features as far as the eye could see, and farther, and as far as even the best human eye could see, or the best nonhuman yet living eye could see. There was only a flat, perfectly flat, brown, smooth, mildly warm expanse of Teflon.

"Is this the Promised Land?" asked Irene. She looked at her sagging flesh, the discolorations, the atrophied muscles. She felt the cracking pain whenever she moved anything in any direction.

"For some," said Glorian. "Yes, Irene, believe it or not, for some people this elaborate monument to waste is the Promised Land. I once guided a young man whose sole desire in life was an overpowering need to be able to eat without having to do cleaning up afterward. The Powers That Be chose him, I don't know why, and he is here somewhere, eating—and even I don't know what he eats or where he gets it—and living simply, cleaning the prairie with a quick wipe with a damp cloth. Look beneath your feet. Even the hardest baked-on stains come clean easily, quickly, without scrubbing."

"They could have made a Teflon mountain," said Irene. "That would have been just as impressive. Or a lake of molten Teflon. Or Teflon glaciers. But *this*, for hundreds—"

"Thousands," said Glorian. "Thousands of miles."

"I wonder if the old people back then knew what we would think of their accomplishments."

"What *do* you think of them?"

"I don't know," she said. "I want to laugh and mourn at the same time. You mean this is perfectly flat all the way?"

"All the way. If you rolled marbles in every direction, when the friction and other physical forces slowed and stopped them, they would all be the same distance from you, if you rolled them with the same force. There is not the slightest incline or declivity. If we drilled six holes in this stuff, we could have the world's most perfect billiard table, if you didn't mind playing on your belly."

"And we have to walk across it to get to California."

"Yes," said Glorian. "No other way. It's a great test." There was a flash of light. When Irene could see again, she saw that Glorian had changed forms once more. Now he was a young woman, perhaps nineteen years old. He was dressed in buckskin—his new form was apparently that of an American Indian of the early nineteenth century. He carried a papoose on his back. Irene refused to be astounded.

"How will we find our way to California?" she asked. For a moment, despite Glorian's resourcefulness, the expedition seemed hopeless.

"You have forgotten again, dear Irene," said Glorian. "I have the Knowledge of the working of things."

"But how does that help? How does Teflon work?"

"Well," said Glorian, taking up a more serious tone, like that of a college lecturer, "you have to understand the basic behavior of long organic polymers—"

"No, no, no. How will we find our way to California if there are no guideposts?"

Glorian looked at her silently, as if she were a nice but slightly stupid pupil. "There's the bridge." He turned around and pointed, as if Irene had already forgotten it.

"Yes," she said, "but I'd like to remind you that the world is round, and that after a certain distance the bridge will be below the curvature of the Earth, and we will no longer see the bridge. We will not have the bridge as a point of reference. We will not be able to turn to one another and say, 'Ah, the bridge is at our backs, so we are traveling in the right direction.' We have to know where we're going."

Glorian just shook his head. "Round," he said. He shook his head again. "Round."

"The world is round, of course. Why else would we have globes?"

"I don't have a globe. There weren't any globes at the training academy. The Powers That Be provided us only with maps. *Flat* maps. The world is flat, Irene, and I'm sorry."

Irene was silent for a moment. There was no point in arguing this further. "Well," she said, "then if the world is flat, and then we'll be able to see this bridge from a long way off, what happens after eight or nine hundred miles, when our eyesight is too weak to spot it?"

"Your eyesight, maybe," said Glorian, "but I have great eyesight."

Irene was growing furious at his attitude. "Do you mean that from here you can see the house of Michael and Constance?"

Glorian turned and looked. "No," he said.

"Well. There."

"There are trees in the way. But I can see smoke coming from the chimney."

Irene kept silent. There was no chimney in the house. She walked away from the bridge. The brown Teflon plain made her uncomfortable, but she didn't know why. It was so artificial—perhaps that was it. It was an artifact. A great portion of the Earth had become an artifact. It was one of the few remaining Wonders of the World.

"Irene," said Glorian, after they had walked a couple of miles, "I have to admit that while my eyesight is really great, it is not as telescopic as I would have had you believe."

"All right, Glorian. I didn't think you could see forever. That's absurd. Turn around again and see if you can still see the bridge."

Glorian did so. "Uh, Irene," he said, "I can't see it anymore."

"I didn't think you could. It's fine. Don't worry about it."

"If I were still in my Aries form, which rules the face and eyes, we'd be in great shape. Instead, I'm stuck here in Libra, and all I can say is that I've got great kidneys and reproductive organs."

"We're lost, then," she said.

"No," said Glorian, "not exactly. We still have the stars to guide us."

Irene squinted her eyes—her old man's eyes—and looked at him for a moment. "You told me that the world is flat," she said.

"Yes," said Glorian.

"Does the flat world circle around the sun, like I learned when I was a girl?"

"Oh, heavens, no!" said Glorian, laughing. "The things they teach people, just to make them feel important. No, the Earth is stationary, and the sun and moon circle it. Just think how hard it would be if the Earth were whizzing around in space. You couldn't even hold on. There would be winds, you can't even imagine the strength of those winds. Everything that stood on the Earth would be ripped away, so there couldn't even be people or any kind of life, and there wouldn't be anything standing in the first place. How else could it be?"

"Then we *are* lost," she said.

"No," said Glorian, "fortunately, over the years, over the centuries, I have learned methods of guiding folk across this prairie.

Don't worry. I've already told you that I've been back and forth across here more times than I can remember. Every square inch of this immense plain is familiar to me."

"That's because they all look alike," said Irene. She began to feel a strangeness in her mind, like a splitting of herself. She had no words to describe it. She put one hand to her head and staggered a few steps. Glorian was concerned, and held one of her arms to guide her. "I feel so weird," she said.

"This is how we get across this unbelievably huge and landmarkless Teflon desert," he said. "The only way. I have become Sacajawea, the Bird Woman of the Shoshone Indians. You have become both Meriwether Lewis and William Clark. "That's why you're so old. Their combined ages were about sixty-five. Now, though, I will use my Indian knowledge and experience to guide us."

"Let me sit down," said Irene. "I don't feel well." There were two more people inside her. Three altogether, if she counted herself, and she always did that. Person No. 2 was Meriwether Lewis. She could feel his presence so intimately that she was shocked and frightened. He was she, and she was he. He was a silent, brooding man. He was impatient, and he had stores of determination in him that would get Irene across the plain without Glorian, if need be. He had a meager medical knowledge that he had learned before he set out with Clark on their expedition to the western boundary of the continent. Somehow Irene knew that Lewis was a slim man, a brave man, a man whose devotion to his dog, a shaggy black Newfoundland, kept the dog alive when the other members of the party thought of killing and eating it. She liked Meriwether Lewis, but he belonged to an era many hundreds of years before Irene's. She liked him, but she didn't want him in her head.

Also there was William Clark. Lewis had asked that Clark accompany him on the journey. Clark was the exact opposite of Lewis. He chattered in her mind constantly, talking about everything he remembered, about the way the plains had looked in the early 1800s, about Glorian as a leader, about Sacajawea, about everything. He was not as well educated as Lewis, but he had been a superb mapmaker. That might be handy if Glorian's powers failed, thought Irene, until she recalled that anything William Clark had put down on a map had been destroyed before Irene was born. Clark did not lose his temper easily, so that while Lewis was arguing heatedly for Irene to let him rest, Clark was enjoying the chance to see the country again, to see new things, to marvel at what was for him the far-distant future.

"I want them out of here," said Irene, looking dazed, "and I want them out of here *now*."

Glorian, in the form of Sacajawea, looked down at her. "Look," he said, "if I'm going to guide us across this desert, I'll have to have ancient wisdom. Even if the maps at the academy have only a blank space here marked 'Teflon Plain,' you'll have to trust me."

"Why should I?" asked Irene angrily, and she realized that she had the support of the long-dead Meriwether Lewis. Her legs hurt, and her mind was still unclear.

"What other choice do you have?" asked Glorian. He was beautiful and young, and the William Clark in Irene had a special affection for her (Sacajawea).

"I'll sit here and die."

"Don't do that," said Glorian. "It would be a tremendous waste."

Irene just turned her head and scanned the everlasting flat expanse of Teflon. "Tremendous waste," she said.

"Don't worry," said Glorian.

"Ha," said Meriwether Lewis.

"Ha," said William Clark.

Irene herself just stared up at Glorian. She didn't say a word.

They started across the plain again. The sun was going down in front of them. There were only a few hours of daylight left, but Glorian didn't seem concerned. Once Irene saw a small round hole, about eight inches in diameter, set in the smooth surface of the ground. "What's that," she asked, and both Lewis and Clark were interested, too.

"When they built this," said Glorian, waving an arm to indicate the thousands of miles of Teflon, "they put in man-made burrows for the prairie dogs. Someone evidently liked prairie dogs."

"I like them," said Irene, speaking the words she heard Clark say in her mind.

"I do, too," said Glorian, "but it's best not to get attached to them."

"Do they taste good?" asked Irene.

Glorian was shocked. "We're not that badly off."

"How badly off are we?"

Glorian turned around, facing the way they had come. Irene turned around also. She could no longer see the bridge. She could only see a level surface of Teflon XVII ahead of her, to her left, to her right, behind her. She was suddenly gripped by a paralyzing kind of agoraphobia. The complete emptiness horrified her. She fell to the ground, spreading out her old man's arms as if to grip the world. She didn't care if it were flat or round, she just wanted to be home.

"I know that feeling," said Glorian, trying to be sympathetic. "I experienced it myself, believe it or not."

"I don't really care," said Irene. Her voice was muffled because her face was pressed tightly against the ground. The Teflon coating smelled odd. Both Lewis and Clark made mental notes of that.

"Come on," said Glorian.

"No."

"Come *on*."

"No. Get someone else."

"Irene, show a little courage."

Irene stayed where she was, spread out under the sky, under the warm sun, with her eyes tightly closed, and she said nothing for a long time.

"Get up, Irene," said Glorian.

"Come along, old gal," said Meriwether Lewis. "This isn't the way to the western ocean."

"You'll never see a prairie dog this way," said William Clark.

When the sun began to set, as dusk set in, Irene opened her eyes. It wasn't as bad then. The hugeness of the plain, the total absence of anything but the nineteen-year-old Indian girl didn't bother her as much as before. Irene sat up.

"Do we go?" asked Glorian, "or do we make camp here?"

Irene saw something sparkling in the distance. It was sparkling bright red as the rays of the setting sun struck it. It was behind Glorian, a few hundred yards away. The tiny flashes of red made her decision easy. "We go on," she said, standing up, groaning as her knees and legs stabbed with pain. Her back was stiff and so was her neck Her arms felt like they hadn't been used in twenty or thirty years. "We go on. If we camp here, I'll have the same problem in the morning. If we go on, I'll get over it."

"Excellent," said Glorian. He turned to lead the way. He saw the flashes of red. "Oh, no. You're not going to be tempted away from your trials and your mission."

"I'm not being tempted," she said. "That is the right way, isn't it?"

Glorian, young Sacajawea with a papoose on her back, chewed his lower lip. "It is," he said.

"Well, then?"

"Never mind. Let's go."

They walked, and as they got closer they saw that the red flashes belonged to a stack of twelve Royal Ruby nine-inch dinner plates. "My goodness," said Irene.

"Not at all," said Glorian.

"I won't be able to fit all that in my bag," she said.

"Another bag," said Glorian sadly. He reached back and got one from where he had taken the others.

Irene took it and packed the dinner plates away. "How did he do that?" asked Meriwether Lewis.

Irene thought the answer back. "He has special talents."

"I wish we'd had him with us," said William Clark.

"Wait a minute," said Glorian. "This is getting dangerous. You've acquired a great collection along our route, and you know it didn't come from *our* side. Put your bags down, and I'll put mine down, and we'll disenchant them."

"Disenchant?" said Meriwether Lewis, through Irene.

"Right," said Glorian. "Disenchant. Just because you were from a century too primitive to believe in such things, don't interrupt me."

"Sorry," said Irene. "If you're going to put two strange men in here with me, you have to expect—"

"Okay," said Glorian. He put the four bags on the ground, and then told Irene to turn around again. Some time later he said that she could look. She was astonished. On the Teflon ground was spread a golden cloth. The bags were in the center. Among them were candles. In the rear corners of the cloth, in golden holders, were two white candles. In the center was a crimson candle, also in a golden holder. A pink candle was placed one third of the way between the center crimson and the upper-left white candles. Just below and to the left of the pink candle was an orchid candle; below that at a distance that made it unilaterally symmetrical was a blue candle. Just below that and to the right, beneath the pink candle, was a saucer with a piece of mandrake root in it. Glorian had incense burning all around the mystical arrangement. A Bible was placed at the lower-left corner of the golden cloth. Glorian picked it up and read aloud Psalm Fifty-nine. When he finished he took a deep breath and made a hand gesture that Irene should turn around again. "All right," he said soon after. She turned and looked at him. He seemed almost exhausted. The golden cloth, candles, holders, incense, and burners, saucer with mandrake root, and Bible were gone. The four bags were lying on the ground in their place.

"You look tired," said Irene.

Glorian wiped his nineteen-year-old girl's brow. "I am," he said, "but it was worth it. I've uncrossed all the glass. It's safe now. But be careful if you find any more. We'll spend the night here. He reached behind him and brought out a well-stuffed sleeping bag and pillow for Irene, and the same for himself. He also got a bottle for the baby he was carrying.

"How did he do that?" asked Lewis.

"Indian," said Clark. That explained it sufficiently for them both, and Irene wasn't interested in a deeper discussion. She put down the sleeping bag and pillow, climbed into the sleeping bag slowly, and almost immediately fell asleep.

"Good morning!"

Irene looked up. It couldn't have been morning. It must be one of Glorian's tricks. The sun was rising in the east, however.

"Good morning!" said Glorian again. He put the sleeping bags away, took two of the packs, and gave two to Irene.

"I can carry more than this," she said.

"I could carry the both of you," said William Clark.

Glorian got another bottle for the baby, Baptiste. "Forget it," he said. "You have enough problems."

"Enough problems?" said Irene. "I didn't have *any* problems until I *met* you."

"That's not true."

"Well," she said, "beside walking across all of this nothing, what problems do I have?"

"Food, water, and shelter spring immediately to mind," he said. Then Glorian pointed ahead of them, to the west. "And them."

Irene strained her eyes trying to see what he meant. She couldn't. "Who or what are they?"

"Bison," said Clark.

"Sioux," said Lewis.

"Her name is Amitia," said Glorian. "I don't know whom she has with her."

About an hour later they were close enough for Irene to see the newcomers clearly. They were walking back across the Teflon plain. Amitia was like Glorian, a celestial, mythical, totally nonexistent personality. She was lovely. She had long blond hair done up elaborately with strings of pearls, and she wore a shimmering gown of silver. She had sandals with cross straps that tied just beneath the knee. With her was a young man, an older man, and a lot of machinery. "Have they completed their quest?" asked Irene.

"I don't know. When I left, she had been gone for a month. Do you want me to run ahead?"

"No, no," said Irene. She was sixty-five, and even though that wasn't as bad as eighty-two, she still didn't like being left alone on the man-made desert.

After a while, the two parties met. Glorian and Amitia embraced chastely. "This is Irene," said Glorian. "I'd like you to meet Amitia."

"I'm honored," said Irene.

"I'm delighted," thought William Clark.

"I'm a little confused," thought Meriwether Lewis. "She doesn't look Sioux at all."

Amitia turned to her two charges. Irene saw that the young man was leading a chain connected to a huge tractor. There was no one inside driving the tractor, but knowing Glorian, Irene suspected that Amitia also had her ways. "This is Rod Marquand," said Amitia, patting the shoulder of the youth. He seemed to be about nineteen, or Sacajawea's age. "And this is his Uncle Zach." The older man smiled at them. He was about forty years old, and it seemed that he didn't mind walking across America at all. Especially with Amitia leading the way.

"What's that?" asked Meriwether Lewis, through Irene.

Rod Marquand looked over his shoulder. "It's a tractor," he said. "It's pulling a trailer, and we have a rocket loaded on it. We're crossing the country to get to Florida, because that's where all the old-time rocket launches used to be. We're going to find a launching pad."

"I don't know what you're talking about," said Irene.

"You would if you had the Knowledge," said Glorian. He seemed to be in a hurry to let Amitia and her companions go by.

"Never mind him," said William Clark. "What is a rocket?"

"It's a machine," said young Marquand. "It's a method of transportation to outer space."

"Outer space?" said Meriwether Lewis. "The only methods of transportation we had were carriages and ships. Where is outer space?"

Marquand, Amitia, and Uncle Zach all pointed up at the sky.

"But that's silly," said Irene. "The sun and moon are only about thirty-six miles across, and about three thousand miles away. Why would you want to go there?"

"Who told you that?" asked Marquand.

"He did," said Irene, in her old man's body, pointing to Glorian, in his young woman's body.

"Well, he has it all wrong," said Marquand. "I don't know where he got those figures, but the moon is over two thousand miles in diameter, and over a couple of hundred thousand miles away, depending on the day and the month."

"Well?" said Irene.

"Let him try," said Glorian. He was beginning to sulk.

"The Knowledge is not static," said Amitia. "It changes to fit the occasion."

"So I've noticed," said Irene.

"What are you going to do with it in Florida?" asked Glorian. "All that's there is swamp and woodland."

"We thought that we can expect help from the Powers That Be," said Uncle Zach. "We're counting on that."

"Don't count too heavily," said Irene.

"You're going into the sky in *that* thing?" asked William Clark.

Marquand laughed. "Yes," he said, "I know it seems impossible, but it can fly, and we've modified it to carry us in a separate capsule, and it can take us from the earth to the moon."

"But it won't work," said Glorian.

"Why not?" asked Marquand.

"Look at it," said Glorian, pointing a slim brown arm. "It has enough fuel-storage space to get you off the moon, possibly, but there's no way in perdition that it can get you out of the earth's gravitational field."

Marquand thought that over for a moment. Uncle Zach looked worried. Irene was puzzled, too. Where were these arguments coming from? One time, Glorian was telling her that the moon was thirty-some miles in diameter, and three thousand miles away. Now he was arguing in terms of hundreds of thousands of miles. The Knowledge. Ha, she thought.

"What do you think, Amitia?" asked Marquand.

"He's right, of course," she said. "I'm sorry. It was something you would have to learn by yourself. I was not permitted to tell you. It was a trial."

"Get rid of her," said Irene. "I've been trying to get rid of this guy for a long time." Again she pointed to the young Indian woman.

"We wouldn't have made it this far without her," said Uncle Zach.

"Have you been to purgatory yet?" asked Irene.

"Oh, yes," said Marquand. "That's all out of the way."

"When you get to Florida, there will be no rocket-launching sites," said Glorian. "It has all been jungle for hundreds of years. And do you really think you could tow this monstrous machine through the forest?"

"Sure," said Uncle Zach, just a bit uncertainly.

"What do you think, Amitia?" asked Marquand.

"I think that the launching pads will be useless," she said, shrugging. "I'm sorry."

Uncle Zach looked up with a hateful expression. "Then why have we been walking all this way with it?" he asked.

Amitia smiled. "Because you wanted to," she said.

"No," said Marquand, "because I wanted to. I made assumptions that are apparently incorrect. We'll have to figure out something else."

"Actually," said Uncle Zach, looking at Glorian's Sacajawea, "it could prove to be a benefit in disguise. It will save us weeks of difficult travel."

Irene found herself caught up in the other party's problems, which for the moment overruled her own. "That's true," she said, "if you can find a way of launching that rocket from here."

"Just a matter of clever problem-solving and calculation," said Amitia.

"That's my line," said Marquand. Irene smiled at him. He was a clean, wholesome, likable boy.

The two groups sat down together. It was just afternoon, and Glorian and Amitia produced a handsome lunch. It was the best food Irene had had in many days. They had Oysters Rockefeller, Tournedos Marchand de Vin, Brabant potatoes, spinach salad with bacon bits and onion, and Crepes Maison almost floating in cognac. They finished with a Cafe Brulot that was absolutely perfect.

"Why can't we eat like this every day?" asked Irene.

"Don't be absurd," said Glorian. "Where would you get your motivation, if everything was luxurious where you were? Why would you have any reason to move on? To seek out new marvels? And I wouldn't do it every day, in any case."

"Quite right," said Amitia.

"Something has to be left for the human imagination," said Meriwether Lewis.

"That surely satisfied one of my hungers," said William Clark.

"What do you mean by that?" asked Amitia. Her tone was so innocent that Clark, inside Irene, could not answer.

The meal was so satisfying that no one could move for a long while. Both Glorian and Amitia walked away, to let the three humans nap and digest. Irene awoke to find Rod Marquand scribbling in a notebook.

"Not giving up, are you?" she said.

"Of course not."

"Good boy," said Meriwether Lewis.

"There are ways around every obstacle," said William Clark.

Uncle Zach woke up and looked at Marquand's figuring. "What a sensational idea," he said. "But let me check your mathematics." He took out a slide rule.

"What's that?" asked William Clark.

"It's called a slide rule," said Uncle Zach. "It makes certain calculations much simpler."

"Ah," said Irene.

"We call them slipsticks," said Marquand. "They're great for figuring everything from electric bills to cosecants."

"I'll take your word for it," said Irene. "What are you planning?"

Marquand stood up, letting Uncle Zach continue to check the math. "We leave the rocket here on the plain," he said thoughtfully. "Glorian is right. If we blasted off we just might make it to the moon, but probably not. The Vanguard doesn't have enough thrust. Even if it did, there's not enough fuel in it to get us off the moon and home again. We have to come up with a startling new idea."

"Do you have one?" asked Irene.

Marquand rubbed his brow. "I think so," he said, "but I'll have to wait until Uncle Zach finishes. He's the real brains in our family."

"Aw, Rod," said the older man, "let's be realistic. I'm all right pushing one of these back and forth, but you have the real creative genius. I never would have thought of this solution."

"What solution is that?" asked Glorian. Everyone looked up and saw that Glorian and Amitia had returned.

"I think we have an alternate plan to our original," said Marquand. "It would mean that we wouldn't have to hack our way through to Florida, after all. We just build a gigantic centrifugelike thing that will whip us in the rocket around and around, and then fling us at the moon. We won't use any fuel that way. We'll have to use just a little to make course corrections, and we'll have all the rest to save for our takeoff from the moon."

Glorian laughed.

Irene sighed. "It sounds wonderful," she said. Lewis and Clark were both too unfamiliar with the subject to comment.

"This is another trial," said Amitia, "and I'm proud to say that you're passing it with a high mark."

"Thank you," said Marquand.

"Thank you," said Uncle Zach, looking up from his notes.

Glorian laughed again. "You want to know the error in your figuring? You want to know why it will never go?"

Marquand was getting a little irritated by Glorian's manner, particularly since it was coming from a beautiful young woman his own age, and it was difficult for Marquand to remember that Glorian was just like Amitia. "Yes," he said, "I'd be grateful for any help you could give."

"If you sat in the rocket's capsule," said Glorian, "and if you had the rocket in this centrifuge of yours, and it spun around fast enough to fling you into space, you'd be jelly on the walls before you got into the stratosphere."

Marquand looked troubled. He looked down at Uncle Zach. Uncle Zach looked troubled, too. "He's right, you know," said Marquand.

"Of course," said Glorian. "I have the Knowledge of the working of things."

Uncle Zach came over and poked a finger between Glorian's well-formed breasts. "If you do," he said, "then tell us how we can do this thing and survive."

"It isn't necessary," said Glorian. "Ask Amitia."

"She has a different Knowledge," said Marquand.

"Oh, go on, Glorian," said Irene.

"All right," said Glorian. "Put yourselves in your pressure suits. Then take your places in the capsule, and fill the capsule with a thick fluid that will keep you from getting squashed by the incredible forces that such a device would exert upon you."

"Unbelievablel" cried Marquand. "Exactly what we'll do!"

"Isn't he terrific?" asked Irene.

Uncle Zach started to pace back and forth on the Teflon. "A huge centrifical sling?" he asked. "How will we build it?"

"The hard way," said Marquand. "Everything we do has to be the hard way, or it wouldn't be a heroic quest. Right, Amitia?"

Amitia just smiled proudly.

"I don't understand," said Meriwether Lewis.

Marquand walked over to Irene. "We get off this plain, cross a bridge—there is a bridge, isn't there?—and cut trees. We use the lumber to build the centrifuge. We use wooden plugs as nails. We'll find something light and stretchy to power the thing, like a giant rubber band—"

"Never mind that," said Amitia. "I was instructed that if you made it as far as this, to provide you with a suitable nuclear-powered motor."

"Moon, here we come!" cried Uncle Zach.

"First on the moon," said Marquand. His voice was very solemn and grave. "We'll be the first on the moon."

Glorian waved in annoyance. "That's wonderful," he said. "But even better would be getting home again."

"No problem," said Uncle Zach, "according to these calculations. Look—"

"Never mind," said Glorian. "Irene, do you recall that you have your own mission to attend to?"

"You're very right, Glorian," she said. "Well leave in a minute. First, though, I want to say good-bye and good luck to these wonderful people. Good-bye, and may God bless."

"Thank you, Miss Irene," said Marquand.

"Please, Glorian," said Uncle Zach, "look at these drawings and tell me if they'll work or not. There's no way of testing them ahead of time."

Glorian looked at the drawings. "What were you planning to breathe?" he asked.

Uncle Zach laughed loudly. "I knew there was something I'd overlooked. We'll cut holes in the tops of the suits and run lines to an oxygen container."

"I will provide a gumlike substance to pack around the holes and the oxygen lines," said Amitia.

"Problem solved," said Marquand. "Now to get to work."

"Yes, indeed," said Glorian.

"Good-bye," said Uncle Zach. He handed Irene something. Without even looking, she knew what it was. It was Depression glass. But it was special, rare glass, a bridge ashtray set in pink. Each ashtray was in the shape of one of the suits of a deck of cards, and all four were still in their original box.

Irene was too stunned to say anything for a moment. She turned to Glorian. "Do we have to uncross these, too?" she asked.

"From him? That would be a waste of time."

"Then, thank you," she said.

"You're coming with us!" said Uncle Zach. "To the moon, you know!"

"Don't mind him," said Amitia.

"You're coming with us!" He grabbed her arm tightly, painfully.

Irene tried to jerk away, but Uncle Zach's body was twenty-five years younger than Irene's old man's body. "Glorian?" she said.

"You're coming with us!" said Uncle Zach. "Isn't she, Rod? Isn't she, Amitia? The rocket won't work without her. We couldn't all get in our pressure suits, and hook them up to the oxygen, and put the gum around the holes, and start the fluid pumping into the chamber without her. She's coming with us."

"No, she's not," said Glorian.

Amitia looked worried. "He's a little unsettled," she said.

"He's crazy as a loon," said Irene. She turned to Glorian. "And when did you stop calling me 'Miss Irene'? I really liked that."

"I'm sorry, Miss Irene," said Glorian, "but during the battle and afterward, it's been difficult seeing you as anything but a man. A young man or an old man."

"Let's let Irene and Glorian finish their own quest," said Rod happily. "Then, on their way back, we should have the centrifuge built, and she can help us. Is that all right with you, Uncle Zach?"

"Yes," he said, smiling, and smiling, and smiling.

"Then it is good-bye, again," said Amitia. "Good luck, and may the Powers That Be bless."

"Good-bye," said Irene. She started walking westward, and Glorian ran to catch up.

"Am I ever glad to get away from that crew," he said.

"Why?" asked Irene. "Did they make you uncomfortable?"

"Didn't they make you uncomfortable? Anyway, we have our own problems to attend to."

Irene felt someone grab her from behind and jerk her around. She gasped. It was Uncle Zach. "You're coming with us!" he shouted. Rod Marquand and Amitia were nowhere in sight. Irene felt angry. She felt that Uncle Zach had overstepped his prerogatives.

"Let go," she said. She tried to make her voice as low and menacing as possible.

"To the moon!" cried Uncle Zach. "Listen. We'll find a crater—there are a lot of them on the moon, you know—and in one of the deep ones there will be a pocket of oxygen. Perhaps it will be mixed with nitrogen and be just like Earth air. Why not? And we'll find a backward civilization there in that pocket of atmosphere. We'll be like gods to them! We'll show them things. We'll teach them.

And they will be ours! We'll build many rockets. There won't be any problems. We'll have the whole moon to use for raw materials. We'll build a fleet. We'll play with them. We'll create organisms, we'll mold them through selective breeding. A new art form! Do you see? Do you see the possibilities?"

Irene was not confused by Uncle Zach any longer. "We'll come back in that fleet, won't we? To conquer the world?"

"Exactly!" shouted Uncle Zach. "Rod and that dumb skirt, Amitia, would never understand. But you—"

Irene, using every bit of strength in her old man's body—which, for short periods and specific purposes such as this, was considerable—hauled off and slapped Uncle Zach. The man looked dazed. He tottered. He looked around himself unsteadily.

"Miss Irene," said Glorian, "that was another trial. Another trial you've passed. I congratulate you."

"Shut up," she said.

"Miss Irene—"

"Don't 'Miss Irene' me," she said. "I've had enough, good grief. I've had enough for a long time, now. I just want to get to California or back to the house of Michael and Constance. I don't care which. Coming?"

"Of course," said Glorian. "You are a remarkable person."

"I'm also disgusted," she said.

"Disgusted?" asked Glorian.

"Right," she said. She stopped and looked at him. "I've lived for eighty-two years. *Eighty-two years.* That's not much to you, but to the people I know that's a long time. And do you know what? In all that time, no one has ever come up to me and said, 'What's it like?' No one has ever asked me for advice. I've been there before them, and yet they pretend it will be different for them. They don't like to see me when I'm old, because they know they're looking at what *they* will look like. I'm an encyclopedia of information that anyone can use, but no one, not one single person, has ever asked me."

Glorian was silent for a few seconds. "Is that all?" he asked at last.

Irene was going to slap him again, but she felt there had been just enough violence in her relationships lately. She contented herself with turning away from Glorian, ignoring him, paying as little attention to him as she would a troublesome gnat, and walking on toward the west. It was getting late.

"Miss Irene," said Glorian. He ran up to her, panting slightly. The baby, Baptiste, was crying. Irene wanted to soothe it, but then she remembered that the baby was just a prop. Amitia, Rod, Uncle Zach, the tractor, the trailer, the Vanguard missile, the Teflon plain, everything was just a prop. "Miss Irene, we have to stop. I have to protect us. We've left what we at the academy call 'The Zone of Protection.'"

"'The Zone of Protection,'" she said. "How will we guard ourselves now? Oh, I'm so afraid." She looked at Glorian like she wanted to hit the beautiful Indian face with a pie.

"Do you know the tarot?" he asked.

"I've heard of it," she said, "in my reading."

"Wait a moment." Glorian sat down on the Teflon plain and pulled out a large deck of cards. He shuffled them and then asked her to cut them. She did so. He quickly spread the cards out in a formation that would provide occult information and protection.

"Those aren't tarot cards," she said.

"What do you mean?"

Irene stood up. "There was no major trump called 'Rocky Colavito.' Those aren't tarot cards."

"Sit down," he said. He was almost pleading. "You don't understand the danger."

Irene sat down again and took the stack of leftover cards. She turned them over, one by one. The ten of cups. The Sun. Al Kaline. The four of swords. The Tower. The Chariot. The six of wands. Minnie Minoso. Cletis Boyer. Tito Francona. "These aren't tarot cards, Glorian. At least some of them aren't."

Glorian was becoming frantic. "Irene, Miss Irene, I know more about the occult than you. The tarot has changed."

She continued to look through the cards. "These are old baseball players," she said. "Some of them didn't even get into the Hall of Fame. Baseball was Michael's hobby before he got older. He used to collect baseball cards. I don't even really know what baseball is. But I know these men do not belong in a tarot deck."

"Look," cried Glorian, "you have the Wheel of Fortune crossed by Bubba Phillips. It's a bad sign, Miss Irene. It's a bad sign."

"It's no sign." She got up and continued walking. She didn't even want to see or hear from Glorian again.

"Look, Miss Irene!"

Irene kept walking.

"Look! A drain!"

One of the drains. She had yet to see one. She wouldn't give Glorian the satisfaction of being curious. She kept walking. Dusk was settling in. Night would fall very quickly on the Teflon plain.

"Don't you want to see the drain?" he asked.

"All right, Glorian, all right. We might as well stop for the day. Bubba Phillips. I don't believe it. How many cards are there in a tarot deck these days?"

"Four hundred and twenty-eight," said Glorian. He took out the sleeping bags and the pillows. They made themselves as comfortable as they could. "Get a good night's sleep," he said. "In the morning, both you and I will be different. I'll be of average height, thickset, dark hair, ruddy complexion, and I'll be even more of a leader. You will be a beautiful young girl. Tomorrow. I promise. You'll see. Tomorrow morning."

"A young girl?" asked Irene, excited by the thought.

"Yes," said Glorian, "with blond hair in braids, and a blouse with a Peter Pan collar, and—"

"Glorian?" said Irene.

There was no answer.

"Glorian?"

Silence.

"Glo—"

Irene had been seized.

Chapter Ten

Down the Drain

Seized, yes, but by whom? Glorian had said nothing, given no indication that there would be another trial so soon. He had disappeared, evidently, and that was his usual habit whenever Irene came up against a trial. What other explanation could there be?

Well, for one, she could have been grabbed by whoever had been putting out the twentieth-century Depression glass for her. Or she could have been abducted by mad old Uncle Zach. Or someone else wandering around the Teflon plain, like the crazy man who didn't like to do dishes.

Irene felt a strong hand holding each of her arms and legs. Two, possibly three or four, then. That ruled out Uncle Zach and the other crazy man. But this world was so odd, so different than anything she had known...

She had been warned. She had been warned, and she had stubbornly refused to listen. And when Glorian had offered the benefits of his experience, she had turned away. Glorian had only been performing his duty to her. He wasn't annoying or irritating when she realized that. He was only working for her. She complained to herself that no one listened to her or used the value of her experience. What had she done to Glorian? She had refused the value of his experience, a Knowledge, a wealth of secret learning that went back centuries. At the first opportunity she would have to act contritely. She would have to apologize to Glorian.

Unless this was a test, after all, and he was behind it.

It was dark, completely black, and Irene couldn't see a thing. She was being carried face up, and she couldn't see the moon or stars, which had been visible when she bedded down. She had been carried off somewhere, inside something, and she felt that she had been carried down something. What did that mean?

"Caution," thought Meriwether Lewis, "but courage."

"Courage," thought William Clark, "but prudence."

It meant that she was below the vast Teflon prairie.

In the system of culverts the old folk had built.

There were people down there (here)? What a horrible life. What did they want with her?

Snap. It was midnight, she knew, because she changed from an old man into a young girl. The feeling was wonderful. She couldn't help rejoicing that once again she was in a young, healthy body that showed no signs of infirmity. She felt and, yes, her hair was in braids, and she was wearing a skirt and a blouse with a Peter Pan collar. She would be willing to bet that she had on white socks and saddle shoes.

Meriwether Lewis was gone.

William Clark was gone. Irene missed them, in a way. She was glad to have her privacy back, but they had been fascinating people.

The change did another important thing. She had changed from an old man into a young girl. A tall man into a shorter girl. She was free. She no longer felt the hands gripping her tightly. She ran.

She ran five yards into a hard surface. She hurt her head and fell to the ground. The floor. Whatever.

"I heard him," said someone, a male voice.

"Where?" said another voice, a woman.

"Put on your light," said a third, another man.

A bright light was switched on, and it didn't take long for the four people to find Irene. They looked at her, and she looked at them.

"Wait a minute," said one of the women—the party was composed of two women and two men.

"Yeah," said one of the men. They wore gray uniforms, and it was difficult to tell one man from the other, or one woman from the other.

"We came down here with an old man," said the first woman, "and now we have a girl."

"A girl," said one of the men. "What does that mean?"

No one said anything. Irene thought of running, but ahead of her she could see only tunnel, and behind her she could see only tunnel.

The entrance to this world of tunnels had to be the drain. In the light she could see that the floor, ceiling, and walls were metal, shiny metal, probably stainless steel. That would be how the people of the old times would have done it, she thought. A stainless-steel world beneath a monstrous plain that nothing could stick to.

"The girl will be just as useful as the old man," said one of the women.

"Grab her, then," said one of the men.

Irene knew what that meant, even though she didn't know what "useful" referred to. She started running back, toward the long ramp up to the drain. It had to be a ramp. She hadn't felt the bumping she would have felt if there had been stairs. She didn't care. She just ran.

She didn't run far. One of the men grabbed her from behind. "Come on, girl," he said. No one had said that to Irene in sixty years.

Irene looked at the shiny surface of the wall to her right. There was a bronze plaque bolted to it. It said:

Above This Point Was
The Hanson Building
Timeworn, Nebraska

What did that mean? It was all so inexplicable. Irene wondered where Glorian was. Was this a trial, after all? If so, she'd be free soon. If it weren't a trial, she might spend the rest of her life—and she was now only about seventeen years old—in the world of the drains.

The two men held her by the arms, leading her, more gently than when she had been an old man. One of the women, carrying the light, said, "We must take her immediately to Delfite, to be judged."

"To the city?" said one of the men. He was complaining. Irene didn't know if it was because the city was a long walk, or because he liked seventeen-year-old girls.

"Yes," said the woman. "She is young and strong. She will be a good worker, much better than the old man."

The second woman spoke. "We must not say anything about him," she said, "or we'll be punished for losing him. The managers will be happy with this young woman. She will work for many,

many years. We'll be able to let three or four old people die. And this young one will bring new blood. New babies."

"Good," said one of the men. "But do we have to go to Delfite now?"

"Yes," said the other man. "Otherwise they'll punish us for having to send out a search party."

"Oh, no," said the woman with the light.

"Yes," said the first man. "Let's get going. It's a long way."

Nothing unusual happened on their journey, and Irene tried to commit to memory everything about the route, for the time when she would have a chance to escape. The one overwhelming piece of information was that every square yard of the tunnel looked like every other square yard of the tunnel. Just as above on the Teflon plain, here there was complete absence of detail, except for the small channels that ran along the base of each wall, and an occasional bronze plaque bolted to one of the stainless-steel walls. They walked down the middle of the shiny floor, too far away for her to read the plaques. Evidently they were walking to an underground city—the idea of such a thing was as stunning to Irene as the existence of the plain of Teflon had been—where she would be judged by the managers.

She waited until the men relaxed enough to allow her to escape. That was the only thing she could hope for. It wasn't much. She had already proved that the men were able to run after her and catch her.

With only the stainless-steel tunnel and the four people in gray uniforms to look at, there was no way for Irene to judge how long they walked. They turned into a cross corridor, one lighted by long, glowing panels in the ceiling. Evidently the smaller tunnel they had been in was not equipped with the lights or they were not functioning. The woman switched off her light. "Not far now," she said.

Irene counted steps. Three hundred steps later she lost track of how many she had counted. It made no difference. They arrived at the city of Delfite.

"Who goes there?" came a voice.

"Recruiting Team B," said one of the women.

"Enter," said the voice.

"Thank you," said the woman.

"Nothing at all," said the voice. "My pleasure."

They went past the small bunker and into the city itself. "We'll take her straight to the palace," said one of the men.

"Right," said the other. "And then we can get some sleep."

They walked through the city. It was the first city Irene had ever seen. It was the most people she had ever seen in one place, except for Maldon, which hadn't been real. There were dozens of streets, all with houses, and streets with shops and stores, and buildings with raised domes and spires. It was exciting. Irene was glad she was there. She would gladly stay in Delfite, rather than cross the Teflon desert with Glorian. She hoped that he wouldn't rescue her again.

They walked past many streets, then made a turn, walked past some more streets, turned again, and in front of them was a building larger than any of the houses. "The palace," thought Irene. They walked up stairs. There were two guards, one man and one woman, at the bronze doors. A woman from the party stepped forward and whispered something. They were admitted to the building.

The four people led Irene to a small room. They put her in the room and then went out, shutting the door. Irene heard several locks clicking. "Stay in there," someone called. Irene knew that she couldn't escape. She made her answer as absurd as the order. She nodded. Then she laughed.

A while later a messenger came for her and led her to the main council chamber. The building itself was made of stainless steel, as was almost everything else in the underground world. There were two guards at the chamber door. The messenger whispered something, and the guards let Irene through.

Inside was a plain, empty room. Empty, except for two chairs at the farther end of the room. One man and one woman sat in the chairs. The man stood. "My name is Monax," he said. "I am one of the two managers. Welcome to our city."

"It's a very nice city," said Irene.

"We work to keep it that way," said Monax.

"You will help us," said the woman, who didn't bother standing. "My name is Cremax. If you work, you will become a citizen, with all the privileges that implies. If you don't work, you will be cast out into the tunnels, where you will wander, lost, until you die."

Irene smiled. There was a certain benefit in having eighty-two years of experience in a seventeen-year-old body. "That makes the decision simpler," she said. "How may I help?"

"Excellent," said Monax, walking toward her. "We will put you on one of our regular work crews. You will be guarded closely, so don't get any foolish ideas of escape."

"I have no reason to escape, as long as my simple needs are satisfied," she said. She smiled at Monax.

"Excellent," he said, smiling in return. "The recruiting team that found you will be rewarded. If you're not lying." The smile disappeared, and Irene knew that Monax was a cruel man underneath. Since leaving the house of Michael and Constance, she had learned that everything had something else underneath, and the something was the more important part.

Irene was led out of the chamber and put right to work. Her job was shining the stainless-steel tunnels. They twisted underground for miles, no one knew how far, but the total length must have been so astounding that even an outsider like Irene would have trouble believing it. Even though this was an immense distance, every foot of the way was kept sparkling clean by teams of polishers, equipped with Scrubbi pads and cans of Jennings' Metal Polish. Irene didn't know where these things came from. Perhaps the old people of the old days had provided them. Maybe they were manufactured in Delfite. After a while, when she became too tired to work, she ceased to care. Every once in a while—some unit of time, some arbitrary unit that was kept by the overseers and unknown to the workers—they were told to stop working. Then they walked slowly back to the city and their homes. Irene had been given a nice, small cottage that supplied all the food she wanted and whatever she requested for entertainment. The only displeasing thing was the great quantity of flamingo decals everywhere, on cupboards, on canisters, in the bathroom, everywhere. The only cost was the incessant daily work in the tunnels, polishing, polishing.

Sometimes she came across bronze plaques.

Above This Point Was
Caffiero's Rexall
Obsolete, Missouri

Above This Point Was
Kendall's Food Store
Antiquated, Arkansas

Above This Point Was
Sid's King-O-Taffy
Primordial, Louisiana

She didn't know what these plaques meant. She had heard of Missouri, Nebraska, and Louisiana, of course, in her long life, but she had always thought they were mythical lands, much like Oregon—that is, places where nonexistent heroes went to fight nonexistent dragons for the hand of nonexistent princesses and half the realms of nonexistent Kings. But evidently she had been wrong all those years. These places had once been real, and the only indication of their reality were the small plaques fixed to the stainless-steel walls of the tunnels. But they were so close together that she doubted they could be true. She found two, separated by not more than twenty yards; one claimed to be below a point in Iowa, the other below Arkansas.

There was only one answer.

The world was round, in fact. A sphere. And she was at the center of the sphere, where the radii leading to points far apart on the surface were close together at the center. But if that were the case, she would have had to have made a long, long descent, and the night she was captured she was carried down no more than thirty yards.

The only answer was the wrong answer. That meant the plaques were false. Why?

After days and weeks of labor, Irene didn't care anymore. She received her Scrubbi pad and her can of polish and did her work, eliminating smudges—there were rarely smudges, no one would think to put a hand to the steel wall—and polishing the floor of footprints. Her life was surprisingly fulfilling. She had a job, she knew exactly what was expected of her, she did that job, and she was rewarded with everything she needed to be happy. At the house of Michael and Constance, she had been provided with everything she needed to be happy, but she didn't have a job, a position, a purpose. This, as tiring as it was, was a great deal better. And compared to walking across the Teflon prairie...

One day, while she was hard at work polishing the floor of a tunnel, one that had a plaque claiming that it was beneath the former site of The Olde Manse Gifts, Venerable, Kansas, there was a great clamor from a side tunnel not far from her. She crept forward and saw that some men, dressed in the gray uniforms of the city of Delfite, were engaged in battle, genuine battle, with men wearing white uniforms. She had never seen white uniforms before. She watched, disinterested, somewhat entertained. After the experience at Maldon, her views on military matters had changed somewhat. She could appreciate bravery now, she could understand the need to strike back in defense of one's own home. That was what the men in the gray uniforms were doing. They were doing it badly.

After a short while there were only white-uniformed men left alive. The tunnel was nearly blocked with dead bodies, and blood ran in rivulets in the channels. It would take a lot of people with a lot of Scrabbi pads to remove the signs of battle.

One of the men noticed her and walked toward her, raising one hand in a sign of peace. Irene thought that ironic.

"Hello, young one," said the man. Irene thought that charming.

"Hello," she said, feeling again tensions in her body that had been dormant for many years. The man in the white uniform was very handsome.

"Will you come with us?" he asked. "The only alternative is death."

Irene laughed. "Let me think about it," she said. "All right, I'll go. Where are we going?"

The man was startled. "Don't you know?"

"No," she said. "I've only been here a short while."

"Well," he said, putting one arm around her shoulders and guiding her past the corpses in the corridor, "we are from another city."

"I guessed that, but I didn't until now know that there was

another city," she said, pleased by the feeling his arm around her aroused.

"Yes, we are from the city of Platonite. We are the caretakers of the Teflon plain. These people here are our enemies because they are jealous, and are always trying to usurp our privileges. We are in heaven, you see, and this is purgatory."

"Oh," said Irene. Being in purgatory twice in one quest was excessive, she thought. "They can't be let into Platonite too soon, right?"

"Exactly," said the young man. "But I have made the decision that you are qualified to make that upward climb."

"On what basis?"

The young man smiled and squeezed her. "Oh," he said, "I have my ways."

"You aren't Glorian, are you?"

At the mention of Glorian's name the young man shrank away from Irene. He seemed terrified. "You are with Glorian?" he asked.

"I was," said Irene. "Until the people from Delfite captured me up on the plain."

"They dared?"

"Yes," she said.

"Then they have paid. That is why we have been sent here. I understand, now."

"How?" asked Irene. "How have they paid?"

The young man seemed a bit bolder now. He felt secure. He came closer. "Platonite is heaven. We rake the occasional leaves that blow across the plain, and wash the occasional hotspot that a careless camper has left unclean. Delfite is purgatory, where by your labor you may be admitted eventually into Platonite, as now."

"Can I ask you a question?" said Irene. "I've always wanted to know the answer to this one."

"Of course," said the young man, once again putting his arm around her. She was glad.

"Is there a hell?"

"There is another level below this," he said. "And the uniforms are black."

"What kind of work do they do down there?" asked Irene.

The young man looked at her grimly. "You don't want to know," he said.

"You're right," she said. They walked on.

The city of Platonite was quite a distance, judged by the time it took for Irene and her white-uniformed companions to get there. She was surprised, and then not surprised, to see that Platonite looked almost the same as Delfite. "We've climbed higher on our way here," said the young man, whose name Irene still didn't know, "and we're just under the Teflon plain. The ceiling above you, the stainless-steel ceiling, is the last layer beneath the Teflon. Lower, in Delfite, there were many feet of soil between the stainless steel and the Teflon. Here we're only inches away."

"Only inches away," said Irene. She sounded as though she wanted to go out again. The young man caught the emotion in her voice.

"Perhaps," he said, "in a while, after you have proved to our leaders that you will be loyal to Platonite, that you will not steal our wealth and our secrets and take them back with you to Delfite, you will be permitted to go out with a crew of leaf rakers or hotspot scourers. Look. See? A drain. Rainwater from above falls through that drain. Now these channels lead to larger channels, in distant tunnels, and then to still larger channels, and then eventually into a stream, then a river, then who knows where?"

"I will be loyal," said Irene. She felt very tired, even though her body was younger and stronger than it had been in many years. She felt exhausted in her soul. Perhaps that was the way that Glorian—wherever he was—wanted it. The way the Powers That Be—whatever they were—wanted it.

"I am glad to hear that," said the young man. "You will come and reside in my house." Irene's expression must have frightened him, because he said hurriedly, "There's no cause for embarrassment or alarm, because I have a large dog that you may keep for protection, and we can get you a whistle that will summon aid."

"Thank you," she said. "I am not afraid."

When they arrived at the house, the young man showed Irene to her quarters, gave orders to his servants to answer any of her needs, and then left to fill his duty for the evening. He was assigned to a leaf-raking team. A Platonite's work was never done.

Irene stretched out on the bed and sighed. She was comfortable, almost obscenely so. It was the first bed she had rested on in many days. And her body! Seventeen years old! She didn't have to restrict her diet or her activities—suddenly she thought about an activity that she might restrict, or at least about which she would have to maintain a certain amount of caution. She shivered.

There was a bowl of fruit beside the bed, wrapped in a clear plastic film. "How thoughtful of the young man," thought Irene. She was hungry. She opened the basket, and there was a card inside. She took out a large apple and began eating it as she read the card.

Dear Miss Irene:

Hope all is well with you. I have been fine, no need to worry on my account. We'll get you out of this gilded prison soon. Have no fears. There are people and powers who have not given up on you.

Arrangements are currently being made to rescue you from your fate worse than death. What a calamity! And to occur while you are in such a, well, nubile form. I have been properly punished, and I bear it with no ill will toward you. Be assured of this, also.

We will meet again, soon. At that time I would like to go over my plans with you, so that this kind of thing will not happen in the future. Your quest is so important that I was distracted by all that glass. I let down my guard, and look what happened! How foolish of me! I will not do it again, so you may have complete confidence and faith in me, as you did in the past.

Yours sincerely,
Glorian

Irene spit out the piece of apple she was eating. She put the rest of the apple back in the basket. She was furious. She got off the bed and called for one of the maids.

"Yes, miss?" said the maid when she arrived.

"Who put that basket of fruit on the table?" asked Irene.

"I don't know," said the maid. "Would you like me to find out?"

Irene hit the wall by the door with her fist. "No," she said, "it probably just appeared, anyway. Take it with you."

"Yes, miss." The maid went into the room and took the basket of fruit. "May we have it?" she asked.

"Of course."

"Thank you, miss." The maid was starting on a pear before she left the room.

Irene couldn't recall the last time she had been so angry. If she ever saw Glorian again, she would—

What would she do? Tear out his eyes? Scratch him with her long, teen-age nails? Slap him silly? Not talk to him? Make him stay home for a month? Cut off his allowance?

There was nothing she could do.

After eighty-two years, Irene had discovered a new kind of anger.

She went back into the room. The whistle had been carefully placed beside her bed, in case Irene needed sudden aid to ward off the advances of the young man or any of his attendants. She knew it was valueless. She walked around the room. She walked around the room again. She sat on the bed. She walked around the room.

She was bored in Platonite.

In some ways, Glorian was right. She hated to admit it, but she was looking forward to her rescue. She wanted to be back up on the Teflon plain, or farther along, near the Rocky Mountains, and then California, and then the home of Elizabeth Dawson Douglas. All that glass!

The glass in her backpacks. It was all at the campsite. Everything she had gathered on her journey was lost, unless Glorian could magically make it reappear, and Irene was of the opinion that he wouldn't care to.

Perhaps this was the result of having the Wheel of Fortune crossed by Bubba Phillips. It was an occult situation, and one she wouldn't wish on anyone, except perhaps Alyse and the real Godric of Essex. That was an unworthy thought. Both of those people would find their own punishments or trials soon enough.

In the meantime, what was Irene supposed to do? Sit on the bed and wait for Glorian's cavalry to come riding up—

"Hello, Miss Irene. I can't actually say 'good morning,' but the feeling is there, nonetheless."

"Hello, Glorian," said Irene. Her voice was pitched lower, she had noticed, breathier, and with an odd accent. She was actually glad to see Glorian now. "Been keeping yourself busy?"

"Sure have," he said, making an uneasy smile.

"What next?"

"We get out of here. I have all your glass upstairs, on the plain, and all we have to do is get out of this house, out of the neighborhood, out of the city of Platonite, out of the system of stainless-steel tunnels, find a drain, find a way to get up to it, find a way to get it open, climb out, and there we are."

"Nothing to it," said Irene. She wished she could have the apple back. She wondered why Glorian had to make things so hard. She admitted to a grudging affection for Glorian. He had always done exactly as he had been ordered, and he had tried to soften such blows as were prescribed. He had done much for her and her comfort as they had traveled across the country.

"Do you think you're up to this now?" he asked. "I've had a quick fill-in on what's happened to you since you were whisked away. Maybe you'd like to have a few days to rest first."

Irene thought of the young man whose house it was. She shivered again. "Isn't there an easier way?" she asked.

Glorian paced a bit, chewing his lip. "There must be," he said. "There must be some old, ancient, gray-bearded plan that no one would be looking for, including our enemies. We'll outwit them. They'll expect that we'll escape the safe way, through one of the drains. But we won't."

"What will we do instead?"

Glorian looked deeply into her eyes. He held her shoulders firmly. "I don't know," he said.

There was silence in the room for several minutes while they both thought. Then Glorian had an idea. He looked deeply into Irene's young eyes again. This time, however, he didn't say anything. He just looked. Deeper. Deeper. Irene felt a tingling in her hands and feet. The strange feeling crept along her limbs. Her body felt tingly. Then her head did, too. She couldn't move or speak. Glorian carried her over to the bed. Then he blew the whistle and disappeared.

The servants ran into the room. They were shocked by the sight of their guest apparently dead. Dead of what? By what means? A poison apple? They could not say.

"This looks bad," said one maid.

"We'll get the blame, you know," said another.

"And then it's gray uniforms and down below," said a butler. They all shuddered.

"She died," said the first maid. "People die all the time. We'll say she died of a fit."

"It was a fit?" asked the coachman.

"Yes," said the maid. "She died of an ecstasy."

"Good," said the butler. "That might work. Let's prepare the funeral barge." They all left the room. Irene was still tingling, and she still couldn't move. What was going to happen to her? Were they going to burn her on a pyre of sweet-smelling wood? What were their customs concerning the proper behavior toward dead people? Glorian just never told her enough.

The servants returned, and a while later the young man came in. He kissed her tingling lips sadly. Irene was sorry that she was dead, even if she wasn't. She would have liked to have gotten to know the young man better. The servants carried her like a large log. They followed a small drainage channel to a larger one, and then a still larger one. They carried her for miles it seemed, until they arrived at a major underground waterway. There was a small, flat barge moored there. The servants carried her aboard. The barge was already covered with flowers, home appliances, gifts for the whole family, and a set of encyclopedias. The young man kissed her again, shook his head sadly, and jumped off the barge. They untied the mooring lines and pushed the barge into the channel. It floated free, and a current took it away. Irene was still helpless, motionless, voiceless. But she liked the smell of the flowers near her. She wondered where Glorian was.

Chapter Eleven

An Unremarkable Murder

Floating on the water, on a barge covered with flowers and small brass incense burners. It was very pleasant. Irene thought that it was the most pleasant thing that had happened to her since she had left the house of Michael and Constance. Floating on the water. She had nothing to do but think.

So she thought. She liked being seventeen again. She liked being a young girl even better than she had liked being a young man; at least the feelings were familiar, even if she had to search her memory sometimes to identify them. She was paralyzed on the barge, but that was really no inconvenience. What else could she do? She could have walked around on the barge, if she hadn't been paralyzed, but that wasn't important. She liked things just the way they were. Peaceful. Quiet. Glorian-less and questless.

The waterway took her for a long distance until it emptied into an even larger, faster-moving channel. This must be one of the major underground rivers, she thought. The lights above the stainless-steel channel cast strange shadows, but they didn't bother her. She was very happy.

She was Elaine, Tennyson's Elaine, one of the characters in one of the fiche that she hadn't read in years. She remembered it, though. Elaine the fair, she remembered. Elaine the lovable, the lily maid. That was fitting. Irene thought that she ought to have a lily to carry, because for all intents and purposes (except her own) she was dead. But Elaine had died, too, for Lancelot, who was too busy with his own business to realize Elaine's passion. Irene made a very good Elaine, but Glorian—wherever he was—made a poor Lancelot.

The waterway came out into the open. She was beneath not the stainless-steel ceiling but a bright blue sky. The air was fresher, and suddenly Irene knew that everything was going to be even better. She could sit up, but she didn't feel like it. She could move, speak, and perform other bodily functions. After a while, she did sit up, and watched the river carrying her away. It was flowing westward, she decided. She turned, and there was no great Teflon plain behind her. There were mountains. She had passed the greatest barrier in her path, the mountains, and she had passed it in the most pleasant manner possible. She tossed flowers from her barge into the water and watched them float. She laughed, but she was lonely. She couldn't stay on the barge forever. Her knowledge of geography was only rudimentary. It was possible that she had already passed California somewhere along the way. But there was no more Teflon plain! She threw some more flowers and an incense burner into the river.

"If only I had a love to doom me," murmured Irene, "then I could be Elaine all the way. But it would be such a pity to be doomed at seventeen. At eighty-two, being doomed is not so terrible a thing." She thought back, and there were no faces before her eyes, faces of men who ruled her thoughts and moods as Lancelot had ruled Elaine's. That was a tragedy as great as Elaine's, she thought. There had not been time. She recalled the bird outside her window at home, and her gentle chiding of herself then. Now the funeral barge seemed horribly appropriate.

The barge swirled into an eddy of the river, and clung against a bank. Irene clutched at the weeds and roots there, and stumbled and fell into the water. She was soaked and muddy, but she was happy. Her life was her own again. She climbed the bank and looked around. There was a great cleft; on either side of the river huge cliffs rose so high that their summits were lost in clouds. "These must be the last of the Rocky Mountains," she thought. "They are mountains, sure enough, and they're every bit as rocky as any I've ever seen." What river she had been carried by she could not name. She didn't know if it were a river of the old days or part of the old people's engineering. She left the barge, looking back at it. Soon it freed itself and flowed out into the middle of the river, which Irene saw became even huger farther on. After a few moments, the barge was lost to her.

Ahead of her, in the cleft, on the same bank of the river, was a house. It was not a large house like that of Michael and Constance. It looked pleasant, though, with bushes and trees shading it, in contrast to the stark and barren landscape in which it was located. The house had but a single story, although as Irene walked nearer she saw that there were cellar windows, too. There were no outside signs of life, such as she might expect near a house in the wilderness. No road. No signpost or mailbox. No lawn furniture. No recreational things set up for children or bored adults. There was just the house.

It never occurred to Irene that perhaps she should avoid the house. Tired, wet, and feeling dirty, she went up to the front door and knocked. The door was a light-colored wood, and by the sound it made when she knocked, she knew that it was hollow. There was no answer. There was a good chance that the last residents of the house had been dead for years. The house could well have been deserted.

Irene found a small button, a doorbell. She pushed it. Again, there was no answer. She pushed it again. She waited.

After a moment, an elderly maid opened the door just a little. "Who are you?" asked the woman. "Police?"

"No," said Irene. "I've just been out walking, and I fell into the water, and I'm cold and wet and muddy, and I thought that I might beg some hospitality from the people who live here."

"We're a little short on hospitality now," said the woman. She was wearing a flouncy white cap, black uniform, and white apron. "Maybe if you come back in a few days—"

"I'd appreciate it," said Irene. "I don't mean to disturb anyone, but maybe I could just get something to eat, and have these clothes cleaned, and—"

"Wait there just a moment," said the woman. "I'll ask the masters." The woman closed the door, and Irene waited. The sun was warm, but not unpleasantly so. She stood in the shade of two large trees. After what seemed like an unreasonably long time, the maid opened the door again. "You may come in," she said.

"Thank you, miss, uh," said Irene.

"Mrs. White, mum," said the maid. She seemed very anxious to please, as if she were afraid of Irene.

Irene followed Mrs. White into a large entrance hall. "Is there any way I can get these clothes cleaned?" she asked. "I really don't want to be a bother or upset the house, but there aren't many other houses nearby to go to."

"Yes, I believe that," said Mrs. White. "Follow me. And remember, we've just had a severe shock today, and the others here are all quite at sea about it, and you shouldn't get caught up in it, and the best way, I suppose, is to tuck you away in the lounge." She led the way to a large, spacious room to the left of the entrance hall. Irene was leaving muddy footprints across the carpet. Both she and Mrs. White looked at the mud unhappily. "I'll find you a robe, child," said the maid, "and then we'll see to your things."

"I'd appreciate that very much," said Irene.

After a short while, Mrs. White returned with a dressing gown for Irene. She took Irene's white uniform, the one she had received in the city of Platonite, and left the room.

Irene didn't know exactly what to do. When the maid returned she could ask Mrs. White about California. This far from the Teflon plain, through the Rocky Mountains, people should know more about California. Irene looked at a bookcase full of old-fashioned, genuine, paper books. She took one down and started to read. It was a strange experience to read something from a large page instead of on the screen of a fiche reader.

"Here," said a man, entering the lounge. He was talking to himself and consulting a small notebook. "It must have been in here, because all the rest of the rooms, except the—"

"Hello," said Irene. She was still seventeen, and that would partially excuse her being there.

The man looked up, startled. "What are you doing here?" he asked.

"Mrs. White put me here while she cleaned my clothing. I hope you don't mind."

"Mrs. White, eh?"

"My name is Irene. I've traveled a great distance."

"Irene, eh?" The man wrote that down. "There isn't anything in any direction for miles. Did you walk here?"

"Yes," said Irene. "I was on a barge on the river."

"The river?" said the man, surprised. "But not far from here the river goes underground."

"Yes," she said, "to the city of Platonite."

"The what?"

"The city of Platonite. Beneath the Teflon prairie."

"People living there? Down there? A city?"

"At least two," said Irene. "Anyway, I escaped and floated on the river, then I got off the barge and came here. Do you want me to leave?"

The man looked at her with a curious expression. "No, no," he said. "I find you quite charming and very refreshing."

"Thank you," said Irene. "I try to be refreshing."

"My name is Plum. Professor Plum. I used to be a professor."

Irene nodded. There was a lull in their conversation. Then Irene sat down again in a comfortable chair and began reading again.

Professor Plum came closer. "I see you're reading Sir Walter Scott," he said. "Do you like him?"

Irene shook her head. Her blond braids swung like pendulums. "I've never read anything by him before."

"Well," said the professor, "if you have any problems, come to me. I know my Scott."

"Thank you," said Irene. "When you first came in, you were talking about something to yourself. I hope I haven't made you lose your train of thought."

"Not at all, not at all," he said. He looked at his notebook. "It must have been in this room," he said. "I've eliminated—"

"Your clothes, miss," said Mrs. White, coming into the lounge.

"You!" cried Professor Plum.

"You!" cried Mrs. White. "I didn't think you'd dare!"

Professor Plum tried to keep his anger under control. "Me?" he said. "If anyone, I'd think you'd be a bit more cautious, especially allowing a stranger in at a time like this."

Irene took the uniform, but she didn't want to take off the robe and put on the Platonite uniform until she was alone. "If you like," she said, "I'll leave. I'm looking for California."

"It's hard to miss, mum," said Mrs. White.

Professor Plum looked at her again. "No," he said, "stay. Beside being refreshing, I think you'd be great help in solving this thing."

Irene held the uniform. "What thing?" she asked.

"Don't you know, mum?" asked Mrs. White.

"No."

"Someone's been killed," said Professor Plum. "Murdered, here in this house, in one of these rooms, and by one of the people in this house. I've narrowed down the list of suspects—"

Mrs. White, though nominally only a maid, took advantage of the unique circumstances to interrupt. "So have I, sir," she said, "and I wonder how my list looks compared to yours?"

Professor Plum only laughed.

"Murder?" said Irene, shocked. "Someone took the life of another person for some petty reason? Murder? In these days?"

"There are crazy people everywhere," said Professor Plum. "Even in a house like this, if you stay here long enough."

"What was the motive?" asked Irene.

Professor Plum looked at Mrs. White, who only shrugged. Neither person said anything.

"Who was killed, then?" asked Irene.

Once more the professor looked silently at the maid. The identity of the victim was not important to them.

"I'm going now," said the professor, making a little note in his notebook. "If you're going to stay, watch out for yourself. The killer is still in this house, somewhere."

"Oh, sir," said Mrs. White.

The professor didn't answer. He left the room and was followed soon by the maid. Irene took the opportunity to dress again. Then she, too, left the room.

The dining room was large, paneled with dark-stained wood, with a large oval table in the center. On the table were three white lace doilies and two bud vases and one large vase. There were a few unremarkable pieces of furniture in the room. There was also a man.

"Hello," said Irene.

The man looked up. Irene thought that if anyone in the house were the killer, this man had to be he. He looked enough like an old-time gangster, a cheap hoodlum. But Irene knew enough to dismiss the outside, to forgo the first impression. "Hello," she said again.

The man was kneeling on the carpet, examining a heavy silver candlestick. "Hello," he said.

"My name is Irene," she said.

"I'm Mr. Green."

Irene laughed a girlish laugh. "That rhymes, you know. Irene, Green."

"Someone could have killed a person with this," he said, standing. "It's heavy enough. A smash or two on the head with this, and it's kiss the game good-bye."

Irene looked at the candlestick. "If it had been a murder weapon, wouldn't it show some signs?" she asked. "A flattening, where it had hit the victim? Blood? Something like that?"

Mr. Green smiled. "You're ignorant of the ways of the true homicidal maniac. This might have been dropped here as a kind of red herring. I suspect that it wasn't, in fact, the murder weapon, but was placed here by the murderer to mislead us."

"I see," said Irene. "And by the same logic, this was not the room where the murder occurred?"

Mr. Green looked puzzled. "That's not sure," he said. "I want to check out the lounge next."

"It seemed innocent while I was there. Anyway, Mrs. White and Professor Plum have checked it already."

"That old woman, and that puffed-up professor, that schoolteacher!" said Mr. Green. "I wouldn't doubt that either of them was the fiend." He got up and left the room. Irene took the opposite exit, and walked across the marble floor to the ballroom.

The huge room was deserted. It was very quiet. At the far end was a raised stage, where an orchestra might sit. There were folding chairs against the walls, and wide windows, closed now, with lace curtains hanging in front of them. The immense room had nothing in its middle, except for one small object. The floor was a mosaic of beautiful stones and magnificent craftmanship, but Irene's attention was drawn to the object in the center of the room. She walked slowly, carefully, soundlessly toward it.

It was a revolver. She picked it up, and then dropped it in fright. She had gotten her fingerprints on the weapon. She shrugged. She checked, and the weapon was empty of all cartridges. She painstakingly wiped the revolver clean of her fingerprints and dropped it on the mosaic floor. Was it another red herring? Or was it the real murder weapon?

Irene wished she knew more about the situation. A few more of the facts, the kind of facts that didn't seem to interest the people in the house she had met, would make the solution so much simpler. Here there were people of the household wandering from room to room, making notes, seeking the significance of an object here, and a fellow resident there. If Irene saw the corpse, three or four very simple examinations would yield enough information to eliminate much of the professor's notetaking. But, for some reason, the professor and the maid and Mr. Green had gone on ahead without this rational approach.

Irene wondered if she ought to leave the house now, before she became implicated. No, she decided, this was exciting, and it was getting late, and she would rather stay overnight at the house.

From the ballroom Irene went into the kitchen. It was a large kitchen, the kind she would have expected to find in such a luxuriously decorated home. Any house with a ballroom must have a giant kitchen, manned by a staff of chefs and cooks. There were no chefs or cooks evident. There was only an elderly woman. The woman looked like Irene herself looked, perhaps two decades before.

"Who are you?" asked the old woman.

"My name is Irene," she said.

"How did you get here?"

"By following the river. I needed someplace to clean my clothing and get something to eat. This house is the only one for many miles, I think."

"That's right," said the old woman. "But you've chosen a bad time to come."

Irene smiled sadly. "I know," she said. "Someone's dead."

"Not just dead. Murdered."

"Do you know how?" asked Irene.

The old woman indicated the various kitchen tools. "Look at these. Meat cleavers. Long knives. Short, vicious knives. Heavy things, rolling pins, meat tenderizers. There are more ways of killing someone in this room than anywhere else in the house. I'm Mrs. Peacock, and I've been here the longest, and I ought to know. You're very young to be tracking down a murderer."

Irene shook her head. "I came just for the hospitality, but this murder thing seems to have possessed everyone in the house."

"Do you find that unusual, child?" asked Mrs. Peacock irritably.

"No, not really. So you've checked and decided the killing was done in the kitchen."

Mrs. Peacock laughed. "No, you little fool, no. It would be too obvious. The instrument may have come from here, but the murder was definitely done somewhere else. I've crossed the kitchen off my list."

"I see," said Irene, but already Mrs. Peacock had walked out of the kitchen and was heading for another room, perhaps the ballroom. Irene wondered if the revolver would change Mrs. Peacock's ideas. She doubted it.

Irene searched the kitchen for something useful and found an amazing thing. When she pressed on a certain part of the wall, a panel slid open, revealing a secret passage. She climbed down the dark, damp stairs. After a few seconds the panel above her closed again. It was entirely dark. She felt her way with a hand on the wall, and the wall was wet and felt as though it was covered with some kind of mold. The great house was rotten underneath. It did not surprise Irene.

She followed the secret passage. It moved diagonally below the house, and she tripped when she came to another set of stairs. She climbed them, pushed open the panel, and emerged into what was evidently a study. More darkly stained wood. More bookcases filled with leather-bound books. A desk. A few chairs. A huge globe in a wooden stand.

On the desk, in the middle of the dark green blotter, was a pipe wrench. "Unusual," thought Irene. She did not pick it up. It was, she guessed, just another false lead. She imagined the murderer running around the great house after his foul deed, planting crazy hints—revolvers, wrenches, who knew what else Irene might find.

From the study, Irene could see the hall where she had entered, and beyond that, to her left, the lounge. She went the other way, into the house's library. This house had more books in it than any place Irene had ever been. Why all the books? Perhaps, in the old days, a lot of books was a sign of something. It was difficult for Irene to comprehend. Hundreds, thousands of books, and the people living in the house could not have had the time, the interest, or the opportunity to read those books. Some of them had once been useful, perhaps, and kept because of that. Others were important books that one or another of the residents thought they should own. But no one, not the most scholarly person in the world, needed that many books. Irene thought it was crazy. These people were keeping thousands of books that no one, ever, would open again. What a waste of wall space! Instead of the books, these people could have—

What? A pastel green wall? Some old prints of works of art that had once existed in the world? No, there really was no better use for the space, and it cut down on the amount of cleaning the staff had to do, and they made great insulation. The books served some purpose, after all.

From the library it was a short walk across the hall to the billiard room. A room set aside specifically for billiards! What a strange thing. Billiards was a game that was not particularly enjoyable. Irene had tried it several times, beginning when she was young, before the age of twenty, in middle age a few times, and once at the age of seventy-four. Not once did she have the desire to play again. Glorian had said that the Teflon plain could be made into the world's most perfect pocket billiards table. If it were up to her, billiard tables would be made into the world's most perfect something else.

There was a man inside the room, knocking billiard balls about with a cue stick. He didn't hear Irene come in. She stood by the door and watched. He was very good at the game. He hit the last ball into a pocket and took a rack and reracked them. He was about to break when he heard Irene clear her throat. He looked up. He was elderly, a senior citizen, but he had a good forty years on Irene. Then she remembered that she looked like she was only seventeen, and the sparkle in one of the man's eyes was suddenly easy to explain. The sparkle from the other eye came from light bouncing off glass. "And who are you?" he asked. His voice was low and husky, much like the voice of Byrhtnoth.

"My name is Irene," she said. "I've come to seek the hospitality of this house."

The old man laughed once, briefly. "I didn't know we had any," he said.

Irene laughed, too. "Something is out there looking for it."

"I've already found it," he said. "You know what I mean, of course."

Irene looked at him, trying to understand his meaning. "You're referring to the murderer?"

"Exactly."

"And you know who did it?" asked Irene.

"Yes," said the man.

"And you're in here playing pocket billiards?"

"Yes," said the man. "My name is Colonel Mustard, and I play pocket billiards at this time every evening. Even a murder and a loose killer are not enough to take me away from my game."

Irene realized that soon she would meet all the people in the house, and that although they all had minor quirks, and that they were all somehow innocent-seeming, one of them *was* the actual murderer.

The man, whose hair was white and who wore a huge mustache, also white, put his cue stick on the table and walked over to Irene. "You know," he said, "at one time, girls like you were daily lunch for me. I was a man of some repute in the world, and I never lacked for girls. But today I have no repute, and still I never lack for girls. But that is because I have a very low threshold of exhaustion. Indeed, my dear Miss Irene, the walk around the table to hold gently your arm may incapacitate me for the remainder of the evening."

A brilliant speech and a wonderful ploy for someone who might be covering up a murder, thought Irene.

"There are no clues in this room," said Colonel Mustard. "Let's take a look in the conservatory."

"What does one conserve in a conservatory?" asked Irene.

"I'll be demned if I know," he said. "Never been in the room in all the years I've been here. This is like purgatory, you know. People, all kinds of different people, come and go. They go after they've served their terms, I guess, and I don't know where they go to. But I've been here a long time. A very long time. My crimes must have been enormous, but I can't remember them at all. Isn't that odd?"

"Yes," said Irene. She tried to wrest her arm from the old man's grasp, but she couldn't.

Colonel Mustard opened the door to the music room. There was a woman, a young, beautiful woman, wearing a dress of Chinese red silk. She was kneeling on the carpet. "Oh," cried Colonel Mustard, "it's Miss Scarlet!"

The young woman turned around, startled. "Look," she said, "I have found the murder weapon." She indicated a length of lead pipe that had no business at all in the conservatory.

Colonel Mustard turned to Irene. "I dare say you've been in this house for some time, eh?"

"Yes," she said.

"And you've spoken with the others?"

"Yes."

"And do they think they have found the weapon, or the room, or the killer himself?"

"Yes, sir," said Irene. "I've seen one person point out a candlestick, and another a knife, and I myself have seen a wrench and a revolver. There are too many weapons in this house, and they're all in places that would attract attention to them."

"Precisely," said Colonel Mustard. "I've seen a rope, too. No, the real weapon has probably been disposed of, and the murderer is one of us, pretending to be just as intent on finding the weapon and the killer. It gets tiresome, you know."

"I know," said Miss Scarlet, standing up from the carpet.

"What are you going to do?" asked Irene.

"I will wait away, and then we will compare all our notes, and together we may find that we've uncovered the murderer."

Irene shook her head. "The murderer will have notes that will lead you away from him."

Colonel Mustard laughed. "Those notes would be too unlike the rest. A simple matter of deduction," he said. "Miss Scarlet, would you accompany me into the ballroom? And you, Miss Irene, there's a secret passage leading from this room back to the lounge."

Irene watched them leave the room. She was alone once more. It took her a few minutes, but she found the panel. She climbed down the dank stairs. Here, in this secret passage, she found a flashlight. She was grateful. She came to the bottom of the stairs and started walking across the diagonal that would bring her up to the lounge. Shining her light in front of her, she saw animals scurrying away. The ancient stones were dark green and dripping. The floor itself was covered with pools of evil-smelling water.

She thought, "Why don't they care *who* was murdered? Doesn't that mean anything to them? And where was the corpse? The only things they were interested in were who did it, where, and with what. What about the victim? Who was the victim? Who mourns for the victim?"

The light from the flashlight picked out a piece of paper taped to the wall. She stopped and pointed the light on it. It said:

Dear Miss Irene:

> This surely isn't the way I had planned for your great quest to come to an end. This is a crazy house. It is a great danger to all who come by and all who seek shelter here. I'm sorry that I wasn't with you, but it was just unavoidable. I'm hoping that sometime, in the future, you'll realize that I'm grievously sorry. I really am.

> There is a certain thing about quests. This house is the last test and trial of all. The people in it are people who have failed their trials at some point. It is a dead end. For me, it is more than that. I have met "my match." I have reached the point where I can no longer be of any help to you. You will reach California without me. The way is clear of danger. Just keep walking westward through the great cleft. Immediately beyond is California. Ask directions there from anyone, and you'll be shown to, where was it? Springfield? The home of Elizabeth Dawson Douglas. In the meantime, I have put all the glass you've collected, all four bags, at the farther end of the cleft. You may carry them farther, or leave them. It is your choice.

> You will recall the matter of the blue Mayfair celery dish. If you remember any of my earlier exploits, you will recall that I am helpless inside blue glass. This is my one weakness, against which all the Knowledge in the world cannot help. I see that in a very short while, I shall be captured. My usefulness to you is ended. Follow this passage, re-enter the lounge, and then run

from the house. Your quest will soon be ended, and that alone makes my sacrifice worthwhile. It has been a difficult time, but it has been a wonderful time, and it has been an honor and a privilege to have met you, Miss Irene.

Yours sincerely,
Glorian

"What?" cried Irene aloud. She flashed her light about, and not far from her she saw something. It was a long wooden table, with a corpse on it, covered with a white sheet. She pulled the sheet down slowly. The body was Glorian's. Irene shrieked. On his head, horribly enough, was a piece of Depression glass, a blue Moderntone sugar bowl. This was what had captured him. Irene knew that he was deathless, but as long as that worthless sugar bowl was stuck on his head, Glorian was powerless. She tried to pull it off. She couldn't. She tried smashing it with a stone. She couldn't. Whoever had put it there, had put it there with more than human means. It would take more than human means to get it off. Irene discovered that she was crying, that she was sobbing so loudly that she frightened herself. She fell to the floor of the passage, and the flashlight rolled away. After a time, she picked it up and did as Glorian suggested. She fled the house.

Chapter Twelve

Out of the Frying Pan into the Foyer

It was night, but Irene fled from the house. She fled alone. She felt more alone than she had ever felt before. She had felt alone before she met Glorian, but she knew that she was not going to be alone forever. She had felt alone in the house of Michael and Constance, but that was different, too. Now she was alone. Her one companion, such as he was, would no longer be with her.

And, after a fashion, *she* would no longer be with her. She had not run fifty yards before another change took place in her. She gave up the young, healthful body of the seventeen-year-old. She fell to the ground, wondering what had happened. It was simple and inevitable enough. Without Glorian, Irene would have to find California in the way she had started. In that body. In that eighty-two-year-old body.

She knelt on the ground—it was grassy here, beyond the house, almost all the way through the great gap in the high cliffs—and felt her body catching up with her activity. She panted. She ached. But, somehow, it was wonderful, too. It wasn't an old man's body. It wasn't even some other old woman's body. It was her own old body, and it fit her better than all the others she tried. She stood up, and she turned around, and she saw the lights of the house she had left. She looked defiantly at them, at the Powers That Be, if they were at fault, at the unnamed enemies, if they were.

She went on, more slowly than before, and when she at last came to the end of the huge cleft, the four bags of Depression glass were there, just as Glorian had said in his note. There was something else as well, and Irene had learned to tell the signs by now. It was a trial. Glorian had said that her trials were over, but Irene knew that sometimes Glorian's Knowledge failed him, or was at least incomplete. There was one more trial.

The road split in two.

One way led down, and Irene could see lights of houses down

in a valley. She could see lights on poles—streets, houses, people. California.

The other way led down into the same valley. She saw lights down there, too.

Which way? It was obvious to Irene, as she dragged the four bags of glass along with her. The second way had a booth set up a few yards into the way. It was a temporary-looking booth, made of two-by-fours and plywood, covered with crepe paper, with signs all over it. SEND IT FROM HERE. IT WILL GET HOME BEFORE YOU. SEND VIA AIR POST. WHY CARRY IT ALL THE WAY? WE MAKE YOUR SHOPPING EASIER—A SPECIAL SERVICE OF. After the *of* there were words that were blurry. Evidently rain had made the letters run, and Irene's old eyes couldn't make out anything.

This was another trial. Just to make it interesting, in the middle of the road leading to the booth, there was another piece of Depression glass, a very special piece, one of the rarest and hardest-to-find pieces, according to Mrs. Elizabeth Dawson Douglas. It was from a pattern called American Sweetheart, and it was a red three-tiered Tid-Bit set, and it was absolutely priceless. Irene walked up to it.

"Nice, huh?" said a man in the booth. "Someone just came by and left it. Told me that anyone who wanted could just take it. I don't know what it is, of course, but if you want it, it's yours."

Irene looked up at the man and smiled. She could take this part of the road down—and then what? Or she could take the other part of the road down—and then what? Someone really wanted her to take this part of the road.

"I'll take it," she said. "Can you package it very carefully and send it?"

The man smiled. "That's what we're here for," he said.

"I have some other things, too."

"Just give them all to me."

Irene hesitated. "I don't have any money," she said. "Can I send them collect?"

"Sure," said the man. "We make it easy for you."

"Yes," said Irene, "I'm sure you do." She took the four bags and unpacked all her glass on the man's counter, then carefully lifted the exquisitely rare Tid-Bit set to the counter.

"You want to insure these?" said the man.

"I suppose. Here's the address." She gave the man the general locus for the house of Michael and Constance, where someone would ride out and deliver the glass.

"It'll be home before you," he said.

"I don't doubt that at all," said Irene. She smiled pleasantly at the man. Then she turned, walked back to the place where the roads came together, and took the other, darker way. She wasn't going to be tricked that easily. The others in the house, they weren't as sharp as Irene—but they weren't as old and experienced, either. Irene had had her trap-sensing apparatus refined in her journey across the country. Her journey with Glorian.

Irene thought a moment about Glorian.

Then she thought that someday he would be all right again. Some Power That Was would rescue him when they discovered him missing, and Glorian would be out leading people to their heart's desire again.

The road was long and twisting, but Irene felt light and free. Her old body didn't seem to pain her as much as it used to, and the thought that before her was California—*California!* Well, she thought, that was better than being seventeen any day. Maybe.

She walked down the road and was surprised to see six men waiting for her. They knew she would be coming. They had bottles of cold soda pop for her, and they had comfortable slippers to put on, and they talked and laughed and made her feel great. She didn't know who they were, and she didn't really care. They were nice men, they knew she was coming, and when she looked at her left forefinger, she saw that a white moon (or cloud) had reached the edge. She was about to become very happy.

The men's names were Tom, Chuck, Denny, Ed, Stan, and Nelson. They lived in California. They each had a separate house not far from each other, and they played shuffleboard and had cookouts in each other's backyards, and talked about the old times. They had had old times, if Irene could believe them. But now, much older, they were all good friends, and they wanted Irene to be a good friend, too. She wasn't sure yet.

They walked on some distance farther, slowly, in respect for Irene's age. "How old are you?" asked Nelson.

"Eighty-two," she said. "Maybe eighty-three. I've lost track of time."

The men laughed quietly. "That's nothing," said Ed. "We're much older than that. We're hundreds of years old, sometimes."

"Why aren't you dead?" she asked. "I'll die, won't I? Doesn't everyone?"

"Glorian doesn't die," said Chuck. "And we don't die. We're being used for something. I don't even know what. But someone keeps us alive for times like this."

"I'll die, won't I?" she asked again. She was suddenly frightened. No one answered her. "You are the Powers That Be," she said. She was a little awed.

"No, no," said Tom, laughing. "We're the other side. We put that booth and that glass up there, knowing you'd use the booth, then come back this way. We're the other side, and welcome to California. This will be your house, for as long as you like."

They had arrived at a large ranch-style house, very roomy and comfortable, and it had a pool in the back, and shuffleboard, and a barbecue pit. And the house itself went farther beyond the utmost boundaries of luxury than Irene had ever imagined.

"I'm afraid," she said.

"Sundowning," said Tom. He seemed to be some kind of nominal leader. "It's a familiar thing among older people. At dusk, when the shadows move, and you see things out of the corners of your eyes, and you hear rustlings, and all around you things are moving, you sometimes imagine that you're somewhere else, that it's forty years ago, and you're convinced, aren't you? you're convinced that your old husband is still alive, that you're still living in your old home in Pennsylvania or somewhere, that the kids are tucked in upstairs. And then, when the truth hits you again, the horrible truth, the truth that you are old, that your husband is dead, has been dead, that your children are getting old, too, and don't remember you very often, and you're in California and not in Pennsylvania at all, it's terrifying."

"I'm afraid," said Irene.

"We're not," said Chuck.

"You're the other side," said Irene. "You put all that glass along the trail, leading me here. You're Glorian's enemies."

"We're not his enemies," said Stan. "He just thinks we are. In a while, the Powers That Be will learn that we're just six old men, serving some purpose sitting here in California, cooking out and playing cards and talking over old times. What kind of enemy is that?"

"I don't know," said Irene. "This is my house? I'm afraid to be alone. Now that I'm here, in California, I wish I were back with Michael and Constance."

"You will be," said Nelson.

"I will?"

"I promise," said Nelson, "if you listen to us. We know the ropes. We've been there before."

"What do I do?" she asked.

"You listen," said Ed. "We teach."

"Tonight? Now?"

"No," said Ed. "Tomorrow morning. Go in there and get a good and safe night's sleep."

"There's plenty of food for breakfast," said Nelson.

"Good night," said Tom.

"Good night," said Irene. She went up to the front door. It was unlocked; the key was in the inside of the door. She shut the door and locked it. She walked through the house, switching on all the lights. She went to every window and door and locked them. Despite it all, these men were the other side. They had done to Glorian what had been done to Glorian. Perhaps for her own good, she thought, but it was still a rotten thing. The house smelled new, the paint smelled new, the furniture had never been sat on, there were no marks or handprints anywhere, the kitchen and bathroom gleamed. A brand-new house, just for her, because they knew she was coming.

That frightened her. She turned off most of the lights and went to bed. She fell asleep quickly.

"Good morning! Good morning!" The six men were standing outside one of the bedroom windows yelling like they wanted her to come out and play. She wanted to sleep. She got up.

"Go away," she said. "Let me eat breakfast, wash up, and get dressed."

"We'll come back when you're finished," said Ed.

Irene rubbed her forehead. "How will you know?" she asked, knowing in advance the answer.

"Oh," said Stan, "we have our ways."

"I know," she said. They went away. Everyone in the world has a way, thought Irene, except her. Perhaps that was what they were going to show her.

When they came back, they all sat around comfortably in her living room. "You know how the Powers That Be have their ways," said Tom. Irene nodded. "And we have our ways," he said. She nodded again. "Irene, we're going to teach you to have your way. Your own way. In everything."

"How?"

"Lesson One," said Denny. "We have inner detachment. Do you have inner detachment?"

Irene thought for a moment. "Not so's you'd notice."

"Well," said Denny, "there. Develop inner detachment. That's how we received you so well. Inner detachment. You're still hung up on snags that got you along the road. Maldon, the plain, the city of Delfite, the other city, whatever it was, Glorian, the house with the murderer. Forget them all."

"I'll tell you why you should forget them all," said Nelson. "They never happened."

"Inner detachment," said Denny. "We have no fear of age, no fear of insecurity. We have compassion, we've invited you in, right into our midst. We've never done that with anyone before."

"You're very kind," she said.

"Not at all," said Denny. "Work on inner detachment. I have a couple of exercises here that will do the trick."

"Oh, do I hate exercises," said Irene.

"I know," said Nelson, "but these will free you."

"Meditation?" she asked.

"No, doggone it," said Denny, just a little impatiently, "inner detachment. Let's go play some shuffleboard."

"Wait," she said. "When is my cycle complete? I had it all straight in my mind when I left the house. The end was here, in California.

But I'm here, and the cycle isn't ended. It doesn't look as if it's going to end for quite a while yet."

"Here," said Stan. He put a revolver on the coffee table. "This one is loaded."

"How much longer?" asked Irene.

"Look," said Chuck, "the whole world is the dream of some guy who's just been knocked out to have his tonsils out. A dream. And when he wakes up, we all go away. His dream."

"Boy," said Denny, "is that lame."

"You create your own world," said Chuck. "All of us. In my world, I live in a great house in California, and my five—my six—friends visit me all the time. It just happens that the six of us men have created similar worlds. But you don't have to. You can create whatever you want, and you can wake yourself up whenever you want, and you can make the world all over again."

"I hope she stays here," said Nelson. He sat beside her, pressing his senior-citizen leg against hers.

"Ah, ha!" cried Stan. "A December-December romance!"

"Listen," said Irene, not moving away from Nelson, "it seems to me that old age is cruel and unusual punishment. I mean, surely making it through middle age can't be more than a misdemeanor."

"So far, you haven't shown much interest in what we have to offer," said Chuck.

"What have you to offer, besides inner detachment, whatever that is, and this old fool?" She poked Nelson.

"Lots more," said Stan.

"We're giving you the world," said Chuck. "The whole world."

"Glorian said I was special," said Irene. "What would I do with the world, though?"

"You'd make it. You'd play with it," said Nelson, putting his arm around her.

"Like a child in the woods?" she asked.

"However you want to think about it," said Tom.

"It seems to me that what you're saying is sort of a compromise," she said. "A compromise between my old opinions and Glorian's, the ones of his that I couldn't accept."

"Fine," said Denny. "I feel that inner detachment growing."

"Heartburn," said Irene.

"No," said Tom, "already, in the last ten minutes, you have grown more than you have in your previous eighty-two years. You can't help it. We're putting up a psychological barrage, and you can't hide. You will pass on beyond us. You will be our master. And we'll force you that way, whether you want to go there or not."

"Look," she said, holding up her arms. "I'm old. I'm fragile. I'm forgetful. My skin is so pale, even though I've walked so far under the sun—"

"In other peoples' bodies," said Ed.

"You can see the blue veins right through the skin. My eyesight again, and my hearing—"

"You're indulging yourself," said Tom. "Stop it."

"I can't!"

"You can," said Chuck, "and you will."

"I can't!"

"You will," said Tom. "Now."

"Not now," said Stan. "We have a full morning. Dancing, now that Irene is here. Crafts. Swimming. Maybe golf. We'll go out to Westfield Villa."

"Shut up, Stan," said Tom.

Irene got up and looked at herself in the mirror on the wall behind the couch. She looked at the familiar old face. It wasn't so old. She looked at her eyes, the eyes that had been clouded over just slightly, the whites that had turned yellow. They were white again. Her hair—it wasn't white. It wasn't brown again, but it wasn't white. It was gray. It hadn't been gray when she left the house of Michael and Constance. And the lines and wrinkles, once so deep they were gorges, chasms. They were now lines of a quietly peaceful face in repose. They had forced inner detachment—removal from the purposeful world, from the necessary, from the goal-pointing of Glorian—on her, and she found that it fit wonderfully with what she had always seen in herself. She felt a flood of happiness so strong that she staggered. Nelson caught her arm, and Irene sat down again.

"You can't stop it," said Stan.

"You can speed up the process," said Tom.

"How?" asked Irene.

"Smell," he said. "Taste. Feel. Hear. See. Wonder. Believe."

"Lean back," said Chuck. "Sit back on the cushions, and let your mind relax. All right?"

"Every time someone tells me to relax, I fight it," she said. "I don't know why. I don't know how to relax."

"You're doing great," said Stan. "Now picture in your mind. Close your eyes. Picture in your mind the world. Got it?"

"Round?"

"Yes," said Nelson.

"Got it."

"Good," said Stan. "Now picture the earth going around the sun. Got it?"

"Yes."

"Now picture the solar system—you know the solar system—in the middle of a galaxy. You know what I mean?"

"I remember. It was a long time ago."

"Picture the galaxy spinning around with other galaxies. Many other galaxies. The universe."

"Trump card," said Irene. "Tarot."

"Get your mind right," said Stan.

"I have it."

"Now," said Tom, "wipe it clean. Take all the stars out of the universe. Every planet. Every chunk of rock. Every speck of gas. A completely empty universe."

"I———"

"An empty universe. A universe-sized space with absolutely nothing in it."

"That's impossible," said Irene.

"Like an attic without anything in it. A slot of space going on forever in every direction, without a thing in it. Just space. Infinite space."

"But without anything in it, there wouldn't be any space," said Irene.

"Great!" cried Denny.

"An empty universe," thought Irene. "This is dumber than Glorian."

"An empty universe," said Tom. "That's the first step. If you have trouble imagining an empty universe, just a universe-sized nothing, you're halfway home."

"You can't create anything in an empty universe," said Chuck. "There's no space. There's no place for God or whatever to create an atom into."

"God can," said Irene.

"All right," said Tom, "God can. But we don't think He would. He doesn't work that way."

"How do you know?" asked Irene. "Oh, I know. You have your ways."

"Now," said Tom, "picture the complete opposite. A full universe. Every single square inch of the universe packed with matter. No space. Forever and ever."

"This is hard, and it is tiresome, and it is pointless," said Irene.

"It just seems that way because this isn't really happening," said Nelson.

"What?" asked Irene, opening her eyes and sitting up.

"It's not really happening," said Nelson. "We're not here, and you're not here. You're sometime in the future, and you're remembering all this. Or you're sometime in the future, and you're making up a false memory, or editing in some of this. This isn't happening now. You're not here. You're not here. You're in the future remembering this. You're not here."

"Final test," said Tom.

"I've had a lot of final tests," said Irene weakly.

"You're not here," said Nelson softly. "You're remembering all this."

"You're losing your illusions," said Tom. "We're stripping them away. Keep your eyes closed. No illusions, All there is is you. That's the only reality. The *only* reality. Whether you're making this up in the future, or remembering it, doesn't matter. You—*you*, Irene— you matter. You're the only reality. We're not here at all. You can't touch us. You can't see us. You are a god who has been avoiding your responsibilities. We're here to force you back to work. In a short while you won't even hear us."

"You destroy the world," said Chuck. "You destroy it when it bores you, and after a time you realize you're a god and create it again. But you have to be pushed. You are the only—

Chapter Thirteen

A Note to the Reader

If, as it was working out, I had let this book end with the next chapter, that would have meant a book with thirteen chapters. I have enough troubles of my own without looking for more. This is Chapter Thirteen. Be content with it.

Chapter Fourteen

A Lighthearted Vengeance

—reality."

Irene hadn't always been dead. She remembered all these things, and she realized that she was hanging in space, empty space, floating, with her memories, and that the six men had been right. She hadn't been there. She had been in the future, remembering them and their words. She owed a lot to those six men. She hoped that they would live long, happy lives in their ranch-style homes in California.

She remembered all the other people she had met on her journey from the house of Michael and Constance to California. Where were they now? Nowhere. There wasn't anywhere. Irene looked around herself in space, and there were no lights anywhere. It was empty, empty space, atomless, matterless, planetless, starless, galaxy-less, universeless space. The only thing it wasn't was Ireneless.

Irene wondered what was expected of her now. Then she wondered if, granted that something was expected of her, who was doing the expecting. Surely Irene wasn't the Supreme Being. She didn't feel terribly Supreme. She felt potential, yes, potential that hadn't been there before the strange, hypnotic exhortations of the six men. Was that an illusion? How much was illusion? Maybe she was in the recovery room, and she'd wake up with her tonsils out, and she'd have a sore throat. No, that wasn't true. She didn't even have a body.

She didn't have a body.

"Do I need a body?" she thought. She liked it the way that it was. She began to hear—how could she hear, without a body, without ears?—a strange, loud noise, a buzzing. What could buzz in the universe, if there was nothing in it but her? Was she buzzing? She had never buzzed before. If something else—and there wasn't anything else—was buzzing, there was no atmosphere for the sound to travel through.

The buzzing got louder. Irene felt herself moving, as though drawn. Moving implied direction, which implied goal, which implied, absurd as it seemed, somewhere else. There was nowhere else.

"Hello, Irene," came a voice. It was Glorian.

Irene was overjoyed. She was so overjoyed that she couldn't answer him for a moment. She was weeping. "Glorian."

"Yes," he said, "and you have work to do."

"Work?"

"The world. I'm waiting, the Powers That Be are waiting, the six men in California—"

"The enemy," she said.

"Well," he said, laughing, "not really, but they're waiting, and Michael and Constance are waiting, and—"

"I can go back?"

"You *have* to go back."

"I don't understand," she said.

"It's your world. Yours alone. Everyone else has one, and this is yours. Do with it what you will. You've chosen to make me, and I'm grateful, but if you didn't, it would still be the same. You are the only reality."

"That's a shame," thought Irene. "If I'd known that, I would have studied harder when I was younger."

She concentrated, and far away there was a light. She moved toward it. She saw that it was a star. She saw that it was the sun. There were no planets, so she made them. All four of them. Then she concentrated on earth. She made continents and oceans. She made rivers and mountains and inland seas and islands and bays and canyons and everything a world might want. She included the Teflon plain, because she liked the idea. She created the cities of Delfite and Platonite beneath it, and a city below it, which she didn't really visualize well because she was afraid. She made everything just the way it had been, because she had lived to be eighty-two and she was happy, and she couldn't ask more from a world.

She looked down at the Earth, and made a moon for it. Then she looked closer at the continent of North America, the eastern part, the part that was all forest. She saw the place where the house of Michael and Constance ought to be. She put it there. Then she created Michael and Constance and Alyse and Man and Woman and all their neighbors, and all the people in the world. It was a difficult job. No wonder she needed such periodic prodding to do it over. "Glorian?" she called.

"Here," he said. He sounded very, very far away.

"If this is all the same, why did I have to go through it in the first place?"

"It doesn't have to be all the same/' he said. "You just like it that way. It could be completely different. We could all be intelligent crystals. But you keep remaking the world the same way. Every time."

"Well," she said, "it must work, then. I should be satisfied. Now, how do I get from here down to—"

"Good morning, Aunt Irene," said Constance, a few moments later. She was not talking to Irene.

"Good morning, dear," said a woman who looked like Irene. Irene watched her carefully. Her—the Irene—voice sounded harsh to her.

"Did you sleep well?" asked Michael, coming toward the table carrying a small cage covered with a white cloth. The Irene nodded, and looked at the cage. Michael removed the cloth. There was a little white animal in the cage.

Irene felt herself stir. "What is it, Michael?" she asked. She had put herself in the body of Alyse.

"It's a baby cat," her father, Alyse's father, told her.

It was the morning of her eighty-second birthday, all over again, except this time she was in the body of fifteen-year-old Alyse. It felt fresh and young.

The breakfast continued as it had that day, so long ago.

"Ask Aunt Irene," said Michael.

"Oh," said Irene in Alyse's body, "she won't help. She's so old, she doesn't remember anything anymore."

"Alyse!" said Michael. "Don't you ever talk like that about anyone! Apologize to Aunt Irene."

Irene was hurt only a moment by what she had said, but she understood it better now. She understood being young, and being old. "It's true," she said sullenly. "She's always saying things to keep me from having what I want."

Across the table, the Irene's face flushed. "I just say what I know," she said.

"That's not much, these days," said Irene as Alyse.

Irene was displeased. She canceled the world.

"Aw," said Glorian, somewhere.

"Don't worry," said Irene. She recreated the world, but this time she was in her old body again, eighty-two and happy. Alyse was Alyse, and she would have to learn everything by herself, the hard way.

"That's enough," said Constance. "Go to your rooms and stay there."

"But," said Alyse, "today's the party at Felicia's house. I have to go over there after breakfast, and help with the decorations."

Irene was enjoying the breakfast, and the relationships, the human relationships. The only human relationships she had seen in the world, from that house all the way to California.

That reminded her of something.

"Constance," she said, "has a package arrived for me?"

"A package?" asked Constance. "Why, no. Are you expecting something?"

"No, no," said Irene. It might be too soon, and it might be that the glass would never arrive. No matter. Later that afternoon, before she forgot who and what she was, she would create a great collection, something that would make Elizabeth Dawson Douglas, whoever she had been, envious. Irene knew that she would forget soon.

"You'll just have to miss it," said Michael. "Now go to your rooms." He was still angry with Alyse.

"See?" said Alyse, as she stood up from the table. "See? It's all Aunt Irene's fault again. If it weren't for her, everything would be fine. She's so old. She's always getting me in trouble. She's always making me miss things."

It would not be long now, Irene knew, before she forgot completely about herself. She would have to hurry back to her rooms. "Alyse," she said.

"Yes," said Alyse sulkily.

"I have a gift for you."

"A present? For me? Why?"

Irene just smiled. Under the table she created a stamp album. "You would like to collect stamps, isn't that right?"

"Yes," said Alyse excitedly.

Irene brought out the album. She gave it to Alyse. "Look through it," said Irene. "Some of the stamps have been collected and pasted in on hinges. There are more hinges, and lots more stamps you'll have to find yourself."

"Oh, Aunt Irene!" cried Alyse, throwing her arms around the old woman's neck. "Thank you, thank you!"

"It is nothing child," said Irene. "Please excuse me."

"Are you ill?" asked Constance.

"No," said Irene. "I just want to go back to my rooms now."

"We'll see you later," said Alyse.

Irene turned and smiled. There was not another stamp in the world.

About the Author

George A. Effinger was born in Cleveland, Ohio, in 1947. He attended Yale University, where an organic chemistry course disabused him of the notion of becoming a doctor. He had the opportunity to meet many of his science fiction idols thanks to his first wife, who was Damon Knight and Kate Wilhelm's babysitter. With their encouragement, he began writing science fiction in 1970. He published at least twenty novels and six collections of short fiction, including *When Gravity Fails* and *The Exile Kiss*. He also wrote and published two crime novels, *Felicia* and *Shadow Money*. With his Budayeen novels, Effinger helped to found the cyberpunk genre. He was a Hugo and Nebula Award winner and is a favorite among fellow science fiction writers.

Open Road Integrated Media is a digital publisher and multimedia content company. Open Road creates connections between authors and their audiences by marketing its ebooks through a new proprietary online platform, which uses premium video content and social media.

Videos, Archival Documents, and New Releases

Sign up for the Open Road Media newsletter and get news delivered straight to your inbox.

Sign up now at
www.openroadmedia.com/newsletters

FIND OUT MORE AT
WWW.OPENROADMEDIA.COM

FOLLOW US:
@openroadmedia and
Facebook.com/OpenRoadMedia